That Could've Been an Email!

An Average Week at a Perfectly Normal Company

I0551573

Copyright © 2026 Joshua D. Whitley
All rights reserved.

No part of this book may be reproduced, stored in a retrieval system, or transmitted in any form or by any means—electronic, mechanical, photocopying, recording, or otherwise—without prior written permission of the author, except for brief quotations in reviews.

This book is a work of fiction inspired by actual events. Any resemblance to actual persons or organizations is coincidental.

All product and company names are used for identification purposes only and remain the property of their respective owners.

First edition.

ISBN (Paperback): 979-8-9944550-4-3

Printed in the United States of America

For everyone who stayed on the call, muted, camera off,
wondering how this became their life.

Contents

MONDAY: "Alignment Day" 1
TUESDAY: "Process Will Save Us" 40
WEDNESDAY: "Visibility & Transparency" 68
THURSDAY: "The Board Is Coming" 88
FRIDAY: "Culture Day" 115
FRIDAY NIGHT: "Poker Night" 136
SATURDAY: "Just Monitoring" 157
SUNDAY: "Preparation Mode" 165
MONDAY (AGAIN): "Lessons Learned" 171
EPILOGUE 213
APPENDIX A: The Organizational Chart (Unofficial) 216
APPENDIX B: Glossary of Corporate Phrases (Unofficial) 222
APPENDIX C: Vision and Values 225
APPENDIX D: Press Release 226

PROLOGUE

The week started like any other. Nothing appeared broken.

Balances matched. Files cleared. Settlement windows closed when they were supposed to. There were open items, but they were tracked. There were owners. The dashboards were green, which I had learned meant stable, not finished.

I work for Applied Systems, Inc. Everyone calls it "ASYS" for short. It's an East Coast company based in Franklin, in the Historic downtown riverfront district, about two blocks down from the local bar and restaurant scene. They have employees all over the globe, including a New York office where most of the finance and investor relations teams work. The company does two things. It processes payments and it maintains bank technology and infrastructure. It started in the twenties as a local savings and loan and evolved into a global banking and payment technology corporation in order to keep up with the world around it. The company is a topic of pride for the small town.

My role had been described clearly by the panel when I first interviewed. The expectations were documented. There was an onboarding deck, a glossary, and a diagram showing how the company made money, and how it moved through the system from the issuers system to the holding accounts. With all of the third party system integrations, and network of bank systems in the mix, the transaction flow looked more like a New York City roadmap than an architecture diagram. I'm continually told that we are just in a "Modernization Phase" for the legacy systems.

Before I turned on the laptop, I figured it would be a week like most any other. Then I hit the power button.

My calendar suggested otherwise.

Meetings had started popping up the previous Thursday, mostly from the executive admin, Tina, all labeled in ways that implied "Quick touchpoint to sync up." Many overlapped two or three meetings deep. Several had no agenda. Some had employees in it I had never met or heard of. One meeting had been moved three times before finally settling into a fifteen-minute window that everyone treated as fixed. My color coding for meetings categories made my week view look like a bag of Skittles.

It didn't take long working here to realize that this was normal.

There were Teams messages floating around describing the week as "high-visibility." That phrase came up more than once, and was even listed as the only meeting description on one of the calls Tina had setup. It seemed to mean that senior leadership would be present to delegate accountability, and that updates would be required before anyone was certain what they were updating on.

Again, this didn't seem unusual at the time.

The first "pre-meeting" started at 7:45 AM.

It was scheduled for fifteen minutes.

MONDAY: "Alignment Day"

Hope dies slowly.

7:45 AM — The Pre-Meeting Before the Meeting

I was already at my desk by 7:30 AM and was taking notes while taking long sips of my coffee that I had brought from home. There was no way I would be drinking the combination of motor oil, mud, and ashtray residue that they called coffee from the breakroom. Rumor has it that the office coffee machine that was inherited as part of buying the building. The machine had already stopped working once that morning and been restarted by Facilities, who referred to this as "known behavior."

Facilities was basically one guy that everyone knew, Jackie, followed by who everyone referred to as his "minions." He was the only one that spoke to anyone outside of this team. They were the cleaning crew, maintenance, and "Masters of Trade," that I would eventually find out meant he was the ring leader of a group of ex-cons that, although now on the straight and narrow, treated every interaction as a favor. If you were able to get him to do it actual job, you owed him. I think it was his way of preventing people from asking him to do anything. He also had a weird obsession with door knobs. A cabinet full of them.

There was always a strong smell of burnt *something* coming from that breakroom. Either the coffee or some variety of fish, Indian food, Chinese food, or popcorn that had been in the microwave about 2 minutes too long, and the smell was caked into the walls.

No one would ask Jackie to clean it.

That favor would have been too great.

By 7:41 AM, the rest of the building was technically awake.

At their cubes, people were already talking about downstream impact of some new company announcement without specifying enough detail to determine the concern. There were references to partner banks, regulatory expectations, and processing constraints that were simultaneously rigid and open to interpretation. Everyone spoke carefully since some execs had forwarded the call to their proxies to take notes for them. Questions were asked in a way that suggested the answers were already known, or at least agreed upon.

Teams was already showing activity, though most of it was passive chit-chat and niceties. The yellow *Away* dot that would come on after 15 seconds of inactivity that acted as a digital tattle-tale kept folks moving the mouse or staying in meetings longer than normal. In the executive hallway, doors were closing as the execs or their proxy started to get ready to join their call.

At 7:43 AM, Eugene, the Co-CEO, joined the call.

He always joined early. It was less about being prepared, and more about symbolism. Being at least 5 minutes early implied leadership. To some of the others, is meant he wasn't very busy and could join whenever he felt like it. It also gave him time to look at himself on camera and make small adjustments, like someone preparing to be perceived rather than heard. He was in his late fifties, always manicured. Salt and pepper hair combed perfectly. Every outfit always looked about the same; button up shirt with heavy starch, pressed black or navy slacks, and either some variety of a patterned blazer or quarter-zip layered on top. His teeth were abnormally white, and aligned so that there was no mistaking them for being natural. His teeth were amplified by the almost orange tan as if he went directly to the spray tan booth after work each day. He felt he was the face of the company, but if that were the case, that face almost looked like it was made out of plastic. And remember, I said he was the Co-CEO. William was not on this call, nor many of the calls scheduled for the day. This was intentional.

The meeting title sat at the top of the screen:

Quick Alignment — Week Kickoff

15 minutes

No agenda.

Eugene smiled at the empty grid, continually glancing down at himself in the lower corner of his screen.

At 7:46 AM, Bob, the CFO, joined. Audio only. Bob never turned his camera on before 9 AM, and rarely after. This had been described as a "productivity preference." No one had ever tested whether it was negotiable for execs to have their cameras on. In Bob's case, it was probably for the best as he had a face for radio. Heavy set, in his sixties, Bronx accent, receding light hair that had been poorly dyed super black, exposing the white, contrasting roots. He always wore some shade of gray polo that was a size too small under a black blazer that was a size too big. It you had said he was part of a witness relocation program after being an informant for the NYPD from inside the mob, I would believe it.

"Mornin," Bob said.

"Good Morning!" Eugene replied, brightly, as if he were being graded on it.

At 7:48 AM, Derrick joined from his phone.

"What's up, team?" Derrick asked, wind audible, sunglasses still on, camera on and facing up at his face as he was walking in an unknown direction. "I'm mobile, but fully here." Derrick was the Chief Marketing Officer. Classic surfer dude from California. Late forties. Sales guy mentality. Everything can be spun. Everything has a price. Tan with an athletic build, sun bleached hair combed back to fall below his ears. He only took his sunglasses off to go to bed. Always wore a bright quarter-zip, some contrasting bright color canvas pants, and a belt that always matches his dress sneakers.

Eugene nodded. This was accepted language although not preferred.

At 7:49 AM, Jessica, Chief People Officer, appeared on camera next, perfectly lit, neutral background, expression calibrated to empathy. Hair and makeup perfectly set. Clothing that looked professionally orchestrated. This week she was a blonde. Last week she was a redhead.

Karen, the Chief Legal Officer and General Counsel, joined muted and off camera, and stayed that way. I had yet to see Karen on camera or in person up to this point. She was the only member of the executive committee that lived in New York, and worked mainly remote, with the occasional trek into the physical office when it was necessary for investor relations, or board meetings. Based on her profile picture, and a few of the company event photos on the company website, she appeared middle-aged, always wore black pant suits, black straight hair, only a little over five feet tall, but very intimidating. She didn't seem to smile in any picture. She made everyone else on the executive team nervous when she was around.

Barbara joined late, apologized in the chat, and immediately began typing without muting her mic. The constant ticking of the keyboard strokes would become consistent background noise until someone who knew how would mute her. This was a normal occurrence, as Barbara was what I would consider a traditional boomer with only minimum technical skills. Her grandkids were tech support at home since she at least knew how to video call them to ask how to work her phone and computer. She would have been on camera for the call, but the camera shutter was closed on her laptop, and she could not figure out why her camera was not working.

Thad, the Chief Technology Officer, joined video and voice, disappeared, then joined again with voice only under a cell phone number.

"Sorry," Thad said. "Dropped and rejoined on my cell. Dealing with a production issue."

"No worries," Eugene said. "Thank you."

Thad was the exec that kept everything running in the background. He was both an executive, and one of the engineers that would be in the server room troubleshooting issues at 3am if a crisis occurred. In a room of execs, you knew which one was Thad based on the t-shirt with some 90's band or video game reference on it, jeans, sneakers, and thin black framed glasses that always needed adjustment. Board meetings were the only occasion you would find him in a polo and sports coat, but even then, if he could pair the sports coat with a sensible hoodie, he would. The board wasn't a fan of his attire, or that he was not intimidated by anyone in the room, but knew he kept the company running, so he was tolerated.

Within the company, everyone was a fan of Thad. He spoke to everyone like they were his best friend. Treated everyone with respect, including the interns and facilities. Even Jackie loved him. No favors required. He had a magnetism about him that I couldn't figure out. He didn't act like an exec. He really didn't act like the other "tech guys" either.

At exactly 7:50 AM, Eugene clapped his hands once.

"Alright," he said. "I really just wanted to grab everyone quickly before the week fully kicks off."

Bob muted himself, which was his version of engagement.

"What I'm focused on," Eugene continued, "is alignment."

Jessica nodded while still fully smiling.

"Specifically," Eugene said, "making sure we're all telling the same story as we head into a high-visibility week."

The keyboard ticking stopped. Barbara now showed as muted.

Karen unmuted.

"To whom?" she asked.

Eugene paused. He smiled the way people smile when buying time in public.

"That's a great question," he said.

He did not answer it.

Instead, he shared his screen.

The deck loaded slowly, as if considering whether it wanted to participate. The title slide appeared:

Q2BoardStrategicNarrative_DraftV7_FINAL_FINAL.pptx

"Can ya'll hear me speaking?" Barbara typed into chat.

"You're on mute, Barbara, but anyway, it's just a few slides," Eugene continued without pause.

There were fourteen.

"Ok, thank you," Barbara said while temporarily unmuting herself, so that it felt like she was participating in the call.

By 8:12 AM, the group were now all fully aware that we board was making a surprise on-site visit this week, and the deck was an impromptu creation by Eugene that he needed everyone else to put their name on to share responsibility. The participation increased once they realized they were being volunteered for the exposure. The group reviewed the slides, and agreed that the word **problem** felt reactive. **Challenge** felt honest but heavy. **Opportunity** felt aspirational but vague.

Thad cleared his throat.

"Before we align too tightly on messaging," he said, carefully, "I just want to flag that we're seeing some intermittent latency in payments. When we see this, it is normally only step one of many worse steps."

The silence that followed was not confusion. It was avoidance.

"How bad?" Bob asked.

"Hard to say yet," Thad replied. "It's sporadic. The monitors are still showing green."

Eugene nodded slowly, as if absorbing wisdom rather than deferring action.

"Okay," he said, before pushing the issue off for another time, if at all. "Let's circle back to that."

Thad stopped talking and went back on mute, knowing that he was just pushed off.

At 8:21 AM, Eugene glanced at the clock.

"Great quick sync," he said. "I'll let you all get to your real meetings."

The call ended.

Thirty seconds later, a Teams message appeared in the **Leadership Team** channel.

— — —

[Teams | Leadership Team]

Reynolds, Thad (8:22 AM)
Seeing intermittent latency in payments. Anyone else?

— Five people reacted with 👀 —

— — —

No replies followed.

Eugene leaned back in his chair. The week had officially started.

8:30 AM — Video Conferencing Is a Lie

The next meeting was scheduled for 8:30 AM. This time William, the other Co-CEO was on the attendee list. The subject was related to new product features that needed to go out within the next week for the payments system.

At 8:29 AM, twelve people joined.

At 8:30 AM, nothing happened.

At 8:31 AM, Eugene began speaking.

"Okay, looks like folks are still coming in," he said, speaking directly into the camera with the confidence of someone who assumed sound was a shared experience. "Can everyone hear me?"

Silence.

Then Derrick's voice cut through.

"You're cutting out a little."

Eugene nodded. "Interesting. I'm showing full WIFI signal." He sat back getting a bit frustrated and concerned since there were more eyes on him in this call. Specifically William's.

"Good morning, gang." William said calmly. "I'm just listening in."

Eugene's normal smile broke a bit. "Thanks for joining, William. Good to have you on," he said, trying to cover the frustration in his voice as the technical difficulties, when he had no issues in the prior call.

William was who the company saw as the real face of the company. He was brought on directly by the chairman of the parent company about a year prior from a firm in the UK, and was previously the president of one of the company's main competitors. He sat with lobbyists, politicians in both the senate and house, brought deals in for the company and told Derrick how to close them and support them. The chairman felt that William could drive growth much faster with the influence he had outside of the company.

William came from money and influence, and was not even fifty yet. Always dressed as if he is ready for a board meeting. Patterned suites, colorful power ties with matching pocket square, matching belt and shoe combos, and a timepiece to match any color combination. His full head of brown hair, lightly tanned complexion, and natural smile completed the package for a full executive presence. It was as if he had a professional stylist always on standby.

His very existence in the company made Eugene nervous.

Bob unmuted. "I can hear Eugene, but I can't hear Derrick. And good morning, William."

Jessica, who was on the call because her department also handled corporate communications, smiled. "I can hear everyone, but the slides are frozen."

"Let me check with my team on the network to see if we can see anything going on," Thad said.

Karen typed something into the chat. No one read it.

Barbara raised her hand. Physically. On camera.

"Barbara, go ahead," Eugene said.

"I'm not sure if I'm unmuted," Barbara said.

She was.

"I wanted to verify that we have passed all compliance checks during testing, so we're good from our side," she said.

At 8:40 AM, Thad dropped again.

When he rejoined, Eugene was sharing his screen for the third time. Thad's team was primary team responsible for the new product deployment. He missed the slides on the product status and action items. Eugene had created those slides without input from Thad, so that he could hit a meeting deadline for the board that Thad was not aware of.

"Do we need to go back over any of the product deployment slides? I was handling the network issue, and checking in on the continued latency we are seeing in the system," Thad asked.

"No, I think we are good, thanks. And quick housekeeping," Eugene said. "If you're not speaking, please mute."

Everyone muted. Barbara muted and unmuted by clicking too many times. Then the keyboard clicks started. Thad muted her.

Eugene took a deep breath and continued speaking.

No one could hear him clearly. A calendar reminder chimed softly across the company. Back in IT, an intern stared at a dashboard that was still green.

Green meant stable.
Yellow meant worry.
Red meant something was hitting the fan.

The dashboard did not change.

The meetings continued.

9:00 AM — Weekly Leadership Sync

The calendar said one hour.

Everyone knew that meant at least ninety minutes, possibly more if anyone asked a question that would result in an unintended action item.

By 8:59 AM, the grid was full again. The same faces, reordered slightly. Someone new occupied the "Rotating Middle Manager" square, introduced as "just helping keep us organized today," which meant they would be blamed later.

Eugene started on time.

William did not attend.

"Okay," he said, leaning forward. "I want to keep us tight and focused. How is my audio this time?"

"Good," Bob stated aggressively, which was his way of saying he was present.

"Let's start with numbers," Eugene said. "Bob?"

Bob unmuted.

"So," Bob began, "from a financial perspective, things are… mixed."

This was not new information. This was Bob's preferred method of operation. Vague.

He shared his screen. A spreadsheet appeared. It had been updated within the past hour enough to show he was working.

"We're seeing some softness in transaction volume," Bob continued, "but nothing outside expected variance."

"What's driving that?" Derrick asked.

Bob squinted. "Hard to isolate. Could be seasonality."

Thad shifted slightly in his chair.

"Or **latency**," he said.

There it was.

He was ignored.

Bob did not look up. "We're not seeing a material revenue impact yet."

The word *yet* landed quietly and stayed there.

Derrick was sitting in what looked like a golf cart at this point, leaned closer to his phone camera and pushed his sunglasses up on his forehead, pushing his sun bleached hair out of his face. "From a brand standpoint," he said, "I just want to make sure we're prepared if customers notice anything."

"Notice what?" Eugene asked.

Derrick smiled. "Exactly."

"I happy to provide details on what we are seeing, so that we can determine how we need to frame any messaging," Thad added, feeling as though Derrick was giving him an opportunity to contribute to the call.

Jessica nodded thoughtfully. "It might be helpful to frame this as proactive communication," she said. "Just in case."

Karen unmuted. "We should not communicate anything unless we are certain it needs to be communicated."

Barbara cleared her throat.

"There is a regulatory expectation around incident disclosure," she said calmly. "Even for intermittent issues."

The silence that followed was longer this time.

"That's helpful context," Eugene said finally. "Let's take that offline."

Barbara wrote something down.

Thad tried again.

"We've seen similar patterns before," he said. "When this happens, it usually escalates."

Long pause.

Bob glanced at the clock. "Do we know that it will?"

"No," Thad said. "But we know that it can."

Eugene nodded slowly, the way people nod when they are simply trying to buy time to come up with an executive response.

"Okay," he said. "Let's stay close to this." Eugene has a series of one-liners that could be used to deflect, redirect, or postpone any sort of accountability for an issue or concern.

The Rotating Middle Manager typed *STAY CLOSE* into the notes.

At 9:37 AM, the conversation drifted.

Declan was on this call, and asked about headcount, followed by roadmap confidence. Declan O'Rourke, the Chief Operations Officer, stuck out in the executive team like broadsword in a drawer full of butter knives. He was brought in my William as his not-so-secret right hand, and some would say, executioner. He was placed as a direct report to Eugene for operations based activity, but was a pure loyalist to William. He ruled with an iron fist, and every conversation felt like some negotiation to keep your job. He questioned everything. He looks for expense reduction opportunities at every level. He was loud. He would also enforce, and amplify, any decision made by William. This allowed William to keep his calm demeanor, as he had his right hand handle the ugly stuff. William was the only person allowed to call him "Dex." No one else dared.

Declan was in his early forties, and came from an a private equity firm in Ireland, working as a senior director in the M&A division, and had worked closely with William in the past on multiple merger deals across the UK. William always lifted him up, to the point that Declan would follow William whenever asked.

"Will this new product allow us to see any headcount reduction benefit? We are still bloated in multiple areas." Declan inquired. He continued without pause, "And are we on track to hit production by next week so that we start seeing the benefit?"

"Declan, I feel good about the delivery timeline, but let's dig into the expense conversation in a separate call," Eugene responded.

"What the hell is the point of new products and features that are supposed to make us more efficient if we can't talk about the expense benefits in the call about the product release?" Declan shot back. He starts typing fiercely into a separate chat and goes on mute.

Derrick asked, "Will we at least be able to run the internal demo for the soft launch next Wednesday, assuming stability?"

"Yes, we are looking good for the demo. My team is just finishing up some testing in the sandbox today," Thad answered.

Thad stopped responding to questions and started responding to Slack.

In the **Payments Incidents** channel, the thread had grown.

— — —

[Teams | Payments Incidents]

Chen, Maya (9:47 AM)
Seeing increased retry rates.

Natarajan, Priya (9:47 AM)
Logging patterns. Similar to March.

Ortega, Sam (9:48 AM)
I can patch temporarily.

Natarajan, Priya (9:49 AM)
Please document.

— Five people reacted with 👀 —

— — —

At 10:04 AM, Eugene smiled again.

"I'm really encouraged by how cross-functional this feels," he said. "Great collaboration."

"I'll follow up with you and William offline to continue the headcount discussion," Declan added before immediately logging off the call.

Eugene's smile disappeared, while Jessica went through some final communications talking points.

The meeting ran until 10:22 AM.

No decisions were made.

The group had eight minutes for a bio-break prior to the next call.

10:30 AM — The Two-Hour Meeting That Could've Been an Email

The next meeting started with glazed eyes. Everyone was already over the day.

The invite had been sent late Friday evening with no agenda and the vague promise of "alignment across teams." Attendance was high because declining felt risky and multitasking felt safer. The audience was the same as the previous leadership meeting, but expanded to also include the next level down management and their proxies.

The new Rotating Middle Manager spoke first.

"Thanks, everyone," they said. "The goal today is just to make sure we're all on the same page."

No page was specified.

Evan, the Engineering Manager, joined from a different room than usual. This was not accidental. It was a defensive maneuver. He had been working with Thad in the background, checking logs, checking connections in the server room, and trying to get more information related to the latency. He had paused in the IT conference room to take part in the video conference.

"So," Eugene said, appearing again, "I just want to reiterate that speed is really important right now for the new product launch. We have committed to the board that we will hit our release and revenue targets, who will be checking in on status later this week."

That comment was the trigger for those on the call to understand what the call was about. Those that had the meeting chat open saw a new list of individuals slowly being added to the call that had any relevant knowledge of the topic, or those that thought they needed to be added as 'CYA'. The attendee list went from 20 to 45 in a matter of minutes.

Evan nodded. "Realistically," he said, "we can move quickly or we can move safely."

"Why not both?" Declan asked.

Evan smiled the way people smile when calculating how much honesty is survivable.

"We can try," he said.

Thad made a blank face in response, knowing Evan didn't have much choice on his response.

Luis, the Application Director, shared a Jira board no one had asked to see, or understood. The tiles on the plan board were color-coded in a way that suggested control. Half of them were blocked.

"What's blocking those?" Declan asked.

Luis glanced sideways. "Dependencies."

"On what?"

Luis paused. "On reality."

"Ok, I can expand on that," Thad interjected before the conversation took a sarcastic and unnecessary turn. "We have a series of decisions that need to be made by this team so that my dev team knows which items are in what priority order. That will help us align which steps to work on and deploy in which order."

"Um, they're all priority #1, and all needed at the same time," Derrick stated, as if this should be a known fact already.

"Yeah," Thad responded, "we have run through this prioritization request multiple times with Derrick's product team leads and Declan's operations leads, and both teams stated that those leads had provided their recommendations to both Derrick and Declan on how to structure the priority order. If everything is priority #1, then nothing is Priority #1. I have sent the request via email and chat myself to both of you asking for updates."

"I don't recall seeing anything related to this. We can take this offline," Declan responded. He would not be put on the spot in an audience and needed to get his details together for a full response.

This discussion was not written down in meeting notes by the rotating manager.

At 11:17 AM, Jessica asked whether the latency issue was connected to the training rollout.

"No," Thad said immediately, protecting his team from any potential negative perception.

"Yes," Luis typed privately to Evan.

Barbara spoke once more.

"If we continue to operate in this state," she said, "we increase our exposure."

"Thank you, Barbara," Thad responded. Acknowledging that her limited participation in the call actually was in his favor.

Eugene nodded. "Totally hear that."

Nothing changed.

At 12:31 PM, after discussions on communications, followed by call center expectations, Eugene looked surprised by the time.

"Wow," he said. "Great discussion."

No priorities were established. No confirmation on deployment playbook was achieved.

The meeting ended at 12:34 PM.

Three people stayed on the call anyway, with two cameras off, because they had walked away for lunch and let the meeting stay up on their machine. One camera was still on, by accident, as Evan had stepped away while in the conference room to continue assisting with the latency triage. In the background, you can see others roaming the hallways that were thought to have been on the call, but were at each other's cube talking about their day. Two coworkers from finance and operations were walking together, laughing and leaning on each other as they walked. Whatever they were talking about was not work related.

This entire feature rollout status could have been a status summary email. More meetings like this would follow.

1:00 PM — Lunch That Is Not Lunch

This calendar invite had appeared late Sunday night from Tina. Eugene nor William would be in attendance. They were set as optional so that it appeared that they may join, to encourage attendance. Since this was not an "Executive" working lunch, Tina did not have it catered.

Tina was a career executive admin. Everyone loved, Tina. In her early fifties. In a previous life she would certainly have been a "Peace, Love, and Freedom" poster child that you would have found at Woodstock. She had an eclectic but professional style, Wild and curly, but well-maintained, red hair with silver streaks, made her own jewelry in her home studio that she stacked with every outfit. She and her mechanic husband raised farm animals at their home outside of town that had a few acres of land. She would occasional pass around pictures of her cows, chickens, goats, and the three pot-belly pigs that she had named "Tiny," "Skinny," and "Bob." Bob was no relation to the CFO, but there was a striking resemblance.

But at work, Tina ran on all cylinders, almost never sitting down. She had seen executives come and go over the years, but she remained the company constant. She babysat the executive's and their calendars to the point that they would not know what day it was without her. In addition to her executive amin role, she was also the primary company event coordinator, charity event sponsor, and any other role that made the company look good in public.

— — —

[Calendar Invite]

Subject: Working Lunch

Duration: 30 minutes

Agenda: Touch base

— — —

No context. Only Tina as the organizer, who was also unable to attend due to a last minute calendar emergency. Eugene needed a driver scheduled to take him and his wife and adult daughter to a K-Pop concert for the weekend. For the team, however, the meeting was mandatory for reasons no one could articulate.

At 12:58 PM, people started joining.

Most cameras stayed off. This was partly about eating and partly about plausible deniability. A few people forgot to mute. Someone crinkled a wrapper. Someone else apologized to no one in particular.

People either brought lunch, or dared to traverse the smell and decay of the break room to try their luck at the vending machine that would drop some generic brand of expired goods, if it dropped the food at all. The large dent on the side of the machine was proof of the frustration of consumers past trying to obtain their purchase.

Jessica joined exactly on time.

"Hi everyone," she said warmly. "I know this is a busy day, so thank you for making space."

No one responded. Everyone wondered why HR had opened the discussion. That usually wasn't a good sign. Everyone immediately started looking at the attendee list to find some sort of theme to the invite list.

"I don't have much," she continued, "but since there is no agenda, I wanted to check in and make sure we're all aligned on how we approach the board visiting this week."

You could hear the single collective sigh of relief.

Still unsure as to why HR is leading this conversation, the Rotating Middle Manager spoke next, already mid-sentence.

"—so this is really just a pulse check," they said. "Nothing formal. We have been in multiple calls today about the visit from the board this week."

The audience for the call seemed to be a mix of personalities from various teams. It became apparent that these individuals were the proxies for their respective executive, and the ones that did not have any issue speaking their mind in a meeting room, regardless of who was in there. This was a defensive maneuver by HR to get ahead of any potential HR violations.

Evan turned his camera on briefly, nodded, then turned it off again. This was his version of participation.

Rachel Kim, a senior financial analyst on Bob's team, joined late from a conference room after finishing up a previous conference call and deciding to stay there for the working lunch. She was the numbers genius that was usually the source of truth for the financial updates that Bob provided in each meeting. Mid-twenties, masters in accounting, rose to senior analyst in less than 2 years with the firm from an intern role. She was always strictly business, professionally dressed, never brought personal life into work. In the conference room camera, through the glass wall and across the hall came two people out from a small huddle room. They froze when noticing themselves on camera on the conference room TV. The conference room was referred to as the "fishbowl" since you could see everything going on in that room.

"Oh—sorry," Rachel said quickly after noticing the two in the hallway. She fumble for the camera button as her face turned blood red from blushing. "Didn't mean to join on camera. Apologies!"

The camera went dark.

No one commented. A few on camera became wide eyed, attempting to make eye contacts with others as if they were trying to communicate through line of sight.

The silence stretched, punctuated only by chewing and the intrusive sound of "someone" typing aggressively, as if trying to demonstrate productivity through volume.

Jessica put on a cracked smiled. Her eye twitched slightly.

"Just a reminder," she said gently, "that professionalism applies in all settings, including informal ones."

Evan choked on his sandwich mid-bite and unmuted, "Haaaa!" He then went back on mute.

Barbara, now muted, wrote something down.

There had been rumors for weeks. Not specific ones. Those were discouraged. But a general awareness that two coworkers, neither of whom reported to each other but both of whom attended far too many off-hours meetings together, were "a lot."

That was the phrase people used. *A lot.*

Their names were rarely said in the same sentence. Instead, there were references.

"Did you see who was just in the background on the call?"

"I thought that huddle room was booked."

"It WAS booked. Now we know why!"

"Facilities had questions."

"You mean Jackie has questions."

Someone unmuted.

"Quick question," they said. "Is this related to the… uh… Facilities email?"

Jessica's smile tightened slightly.

"Facilities sends a lot of emails," she said. "I wouldn't over-index on any single one."

No one asked a follow-up.

The Rotating Middle Manager cleared their throat.

"So," they said, "just to level-set, this is a reminder that we should all be mindful of optics. Especially when the board arrives."

Optics was one of those words that did a lot of work without ever specifying the task.

At 1:15 PM, Declan joined. "Why am I on this call?"

"This was more of an FYI for you that it was taking place since you had team members impacted. You were set as optional, "Jessica responded.

Declan left the call without another word.

At 1:17 PM, a Teams notification pinged across several screens.

— — —

[Teams | Company Announcements]

Facilities (1:17 PM)
Reminder: Please reserve conference rooms and huddle rooms accurately and vacate promptly after meetings. Private use of shared spaces does NOT comply with company policy.

— — —

There were no reactions. There we a myriad of reactions across separate, private chats.

At 1:19 PM, Jessica spoke again.

"It feels like we can use this time to level set on behavior expectations during this afternoon's events. Please be sure your respective areas are clean, all confidential paperwork and materials are put away, you are in business casual attire, and conversations are professional and work related. Please ensure you convey the message to your respective teams. There are a few on this call that I know are comfortable speaking to their teams about such matters."

She paused, hoping for a response from someone. There were a few thumbs up emojis posted.

"If anyone has questions," she said, "my door is always open."

This was metaphorical. Her door, nor her calendar, were open. Not because she didn't care. She just didn't have enough medication to handle the volume of issues that were continually brought to her when the calendar had space, or her door was left open. "Drive-by" HR issues were normally the most severe, since they were normally meant to avoid a paper trail.

At 1:21 PM, the meeting ended early.

Several people stayed on the call anyway, using the time blocked on their calendar to as cover to prevent being added to other impromptu meetings.

In a different channel, someone typed:

Did you hear?

No one replied.

The working lunch was over. Many would now take an actual lunch for at least the next hour.

3:00 PM — Compliance Says Hi

Barbara sent an email.

She had considered a Teams message and decided against it.

— — —

[Email]

From: Hensley, Barbara
Subject: Minor Compliance Observation

Hi all,

Flagging a potential compliance reporting issue related to intermittent processing delays. This is likely manageable if addressed promptly. I'd be happy to discuss.

Best,
Barbara Hensley
Chief Compliance Officer

— — —

No one replied.

Thad rolled his eyes.

This was not minor.

3:12 PM — Meanwhile, in Reality

By 3:12 PM, Thad had stopped attending meetings.

This was not a decision so much as capacity constraints. Status meetings, planning meetings, production support meetings, and latency investigation.

He was still present everywhere he was expected to be. Teams red dot active as "Busy," calendar blocks intact, but his attention had shifted to the only place where new information appeared without preamble.

The dashboards had not turned red.

They had stayed green while systems behaved differently.

This was worse. If you have worked in tech, you know the ghosts in the machine are worse when they don't impact the monitors. It would be even worse if they fix themselves with no help from the team, leaving the group with no explanation as to what just happened.

Maya noticed first and posted to a private chat with Priya and Thad.

— — —

[Teams | Private Chat]

Maya (3:12 PM)
Retry rates climbing. Infra looks stable, but traffic patterns aren't normal.

Priya (3:12 PM)
Auth timeouts propagating. Signature matches March.

Priya (3:13 PM)
That one escalated quickly.

Thad (3:15 PM)
Let me open a channel to discuss as a group.

— — —

Thad maximized Teams and created a new channel, "**Payments War Room – Lite**," inviting his Tech and Security teams. That name mattered. Calling it only a war room would have triggered visibility and immediate forwarding and escalations as the normal CYA protocol. *Lite* suggested more curiosity than urgency.

People joined without being invited.

Sam was already typing.

— — —

[Teams | Payments War Room – Lite]

Ortega, Sam (3:20 PM)
I can put a temporary throttle in place.
It's duct tape, but it'll work.

— Chen, Maya reacted with 👍 —

Reynolds, Thad (3:23 PM)
Assume leadership wants two outcomes:
1) It doesn't get worse
2) They don't have to explain it yet

— — —

No one disagreed.

3:26 PM — A Reasonable Question

Someone new was in the channel. The Intern.

They hadn't been intentionally invited. Thad had invited the attendees by group vs individually. They were there because the documentation said the channel labelled War Room was where questions went. They assumed it meant this one.

They had been reviewing logs because the runbook instructed them to. The runbook was old, but it was very detailed, which made it somewhat trustworthy.

Something didn't align.

They scrolled back through historical changes in the runbooks. Then further. Then further still.

After deleting and retyping twice, they posted.

— — —

[Teams | Payments War Room – Lite]

Intern (2:10 PM)
Quick question — are we expecting retry storms from the training environment to be hitting production?

— The channel paused. —

Ortega, Sam (2:13 PM)
No. Who are you?

Chen, Maya (2:13 PM)
And, why?

Intern (2:15 PM)
Sorry, I'm a new intern on Luis' team. I was told to ask questions here. But the retries look like they're originating

in the training environment, with the config pointing to production. You can tell because there is no '-trn' suffix on the endpoint.
They started right after the deploy this morning.

— — —

No one accused them of anything.

That was the moment things became serious.

Sam pulled logs.

Priya cross-referenced timestamps.

Maya opened a dashboard she had hoped not to need today.

Thad leaned back.

"Oooooh, damn," he said quietly.

3:41 PM — Controlled Panic

This was material.

Not necessarily failure.

It uncovered gaps in the network, deployment process, and access rights.

This would require translation.

Escalate too early and executive leadership intervenes.

Namely Eugene, Declan, and William.

Escalate too late and leadership asks why no one spoke up.

Sam proposed a workaround.

— — —

[Teams | Payments War Room – Lite]

Ortega, Sam (3:45 PM)
I can isolate sandbox traffic and reroute.
Violates best practices, though.
But prevents customer impact.

Chen, Maya (3:45 PM)
Do it.

Natarajan, Priya (3:46 PM)
Document everything.
Especially the decision to do this. I'll need a change ticket to approve from a security standpoint.

Intern (3:47 PM)
…
I followed the runbook for that deployment.

Reynolds, Thad (3:49 PM)
Nah, that's on us. We got it.

Alvarez, Luis (3:50 PM)
I'll have Noah work on a hotfix.

— — —

Thad knew how this would age.

4:08 PM — Executive Update (Draft)

While Noah patched the applicable code files, Thad drafted an email that he would delete three versions of, before keeping the fourth.

— — —

[Email]

From: Raynolds, Thad
To: Executive Team
Subject: Executive Update — Draft

Summary

Teams are observing intermittent latency associated with internal testing traffic. No confirmed customer impact at this time. Mitigations are in progress.

Thad – CTO

— — —

He stared at it.

Too specific.

He revised. Revised Again. And Revised Again.

— — —

[Email]

From: Raynolds, Thad
To: Executive Team
Subject: Executive Update

Summary

We are monitoring a performance variance tied to internal activity. Customer experience remains stable. Teams are aligned on next steps.

Thad – CTO

— — —

He shared the text to the channel.

Maya reacted 👍

Priya added: *Include compliance visibility.*

Sam said nothing, which meant approval.

The intern removed a reaction they hadn't meant to add.

5:02 PM — Stability Achieved

The workaround held.

Traffic normalized.

Retries flattened.

Dashboards stayed green. *Still.*

Which meant the story was now optional, but investigation had to continue.

Sam sent a direct message to the intern

— — —

[Teams | Ortega, Sam]

Ortega, Sam (5:05 PM)
Good catch earlier.
DON'T mention it in any meetings.

Intern (5:05 PM)
Okay.

Ortega, Sam (5:06 PM)
Dude, seriously. I mean it.

Intern (5:07 PM)
OKAY!

— — —

Priya uploaded a document titled:

Risk Summary — Informational

No one outside IT would open it.

Which was ideal.

5:45 PM — Postmortem Draft #1

The postmortem appeared in the shared drive at 5:47 PM.

It was labeled **DRAFT**, which meant it would survive unchanged.

— — —

[Document]

Incident Summary
Intermittent latency observed in payment processing flows.

Impact
Minimal.
Some retries experienced.
No confirmed customer data issues.

Root Cause
Multiple contributing factors related to internal activity and system behavior.

Detection
Identified through monitoring and team observation.

Response
Teams collaborated to implement mitigations and restore stability.

What Went Well

- Cross-functional alignment
- Rapid response
- Effective communication

What Could Be Improved

- Change visibility
- Process clarity

- Training adherence

Action Items

- Review sandbox access controls
- Update runbooks
- Improve monitoring granularity

Owner
TBD

— — —

The intern read it twice.

They recognized every sentence.

No names mentioned.

At 5:59 PM, Eugene reacted to the Teams update with a thumbs-up.

At 6:02 PM, Bob asked if the issue was "material." Declan gave a thumbs up to the question.

The system stayed online.

Responsible parties did not.

As the intern was packing up, they noticed two employees coming from one of the hallway utility closets, straightening their clothing, brushing their hair, and fixing makeup as they walked out. They noticed the intern looking and rush off faster, realizing they had just gotten caught.

TUESDAY: "Process Will Save Us"

It did not.

8:00 AM — Training Day Begins

The invite had been sent two weeks earlier and ignored until it became unavoidable.

— — —

[Calendar Invite]

Title: Professional Boundaries & Operational Excellence
Organizer: Human Resources
Time: 9:00 AM – 5:00 PM
Location: Large Conference Room A
Attendees: Finance, Operations
Required: Yes
Recording: No

— — —

This was noted.

Attendance was high, but did not include Bob or Declan.

Finance arrived first, carrying notebooks they would not open. Operations followed, already tired in a way that suggested accumulated burnout. Everyone chose seats with the care, mainly close to the exit, or at least out of line-of-sight from the speaker.

At the front of the room, a large, widescreen TV displayed a video conference grid.

Jessica was in the back of the room, smiling warmly as a greeting to those that joined. The class would be led by a third-party training company, with introductions by Emily Foster, the HR business partner.

Two other obligatory senior leaders from Ops and Finance appeared as small rectangles in the corner, cameras on, sound muted, so that the group had leadership presence without leadership accountability. They nodded occasionally, as if attending through muscle memory rather than obligation.

In the room, the intern stood near the podium, laptop open, cables already tested. Their badge read **Tech Support**, which felt safer than their actual role. They had tested the deck display three times and still did not trust it.

At 8:03 AM, the door opened.

Two coworkers, not ironically from the two specific departments the training was setup for, walked in together. Alex Donnelly and Jordan Feldman. Alex was the Senior Director of Finance, reporting directly to Bob, She was maybe mid-thirties, but in good shape, and had a presence about her that made it feel like she was once the head cheerleader in high school. Her personality made it seem as though the term *consequence* didn't register. She was wearing an outfit that tested the boundaries of Jessica's patience and the restraint of the men's eyes in the room. The black skirt too short and too tight. The black high heels about 2 inches too tall. The white blouse about a size too small, unbuttoned one button too many.

Jordan had an equal "previous high school quarterback" vibe. He was an analyst somewhere in the operations department. He was in his late twenties, but tanned, short brown hair combed back, and in peak physical condition. He either took notes from Alex on wearing clothing one size too small, or that was one of the traits that made her like him. If not seen in the finance department, you could usually find him hanging around other girls in the marketing department. He was rarely at his own cube.

They were mid-conversation, talking about their "separate" weekend plans with her husband and his girlfriend, smiling, close enough to require adjustment once they noticed other people were present. They chose seats next to each other without discussion.

Then they made eye contact the intern standing behind the podium.

There was an uncomfortable pause.

Not long—just long enough to register.

Their smiles vanished. Conversation stopped. One of them coughed. The other checked their phone. They separated by exactly one chair, the corporate equivalent of plausible deniability.

The intern pretended not to notice.

Everyone else noticed.

Jessica's eye twitched.

8:07 AM — The Deck

The first slide appeared

Our Commitment to Professional Excellence

The font was confident. The message was vague.

Emily's voice filled the room from the speakers with a high-pitched, almost mousy squeak, in a tone that was sugary sweet.

"Good morning, everyone. Thank you for making the time to be here—in person. Hee hee."

She smiled slightly harder on the last two words, with a giggle that would have sounded forced by anyone else.

"I want to be very clear," she continued. "This session is not punitive."

No one believed her. No one challenged her. A few attendees apparently in the know scanned across the room, and paused on the Alex and Jordan, separated by exactly one chair. The two started glowing a unique shade of tanned red that was noticeable by those that knew to pay attention. Some eyes moved to the back of the room to see Jessica nodding in agreement to the message.

Reading from Emily's cue cards, "This is about alignment, clarity, and shared expectations."

Several people wrote those words down without intending to revisit them.

The third party facilitator took over in the room, cheerful in the way people are when they know they won't be blamed. They were hired as a training vendor to serve as an objective presenter that could answer questions in the most generic way possible, to prevent any targeted conversations about anyone in the room.

"Thank you, Emily. Sometimes," the new presenter said, while pointing to the intern to advance the slide, "lines can blur in high-performing environments."

The two coworkers did not look at each other. Her phone became very interesting to her, while he jotted notes about nothing on his notepad.

The intern advanced the slide.

9:30 AM — Training Continues (All Day)

Fast forward an hour and a half, and a few team exercises later, the training did not escalate.

It orbited around the same level of discomfort.

Modules transitioned seamlessly from **Professional Conduct** to **Ethics in Practice** to **Optics and Organizational Trust**. Each section was careful to remain hypothetical while still landing uncomfortably close to lived experience.

Every example began with:

"Imagine a scenario…"

No one imagined very hard.

During a section on *Perception*, the facilitator asked:

"How might this look to someone outside the situation?"

In the back row, Alex and Jordan exchanged a glance.

It lasted half a second too long.

They noticed the intern noticing.

Both looked away immediately, as if caught by a motion sensor. During each group exercise, the two made sure not to be in the same group.

The intern adjusted the HDMI cable, suddenly very interested in the floor.

10:02 AM — Breakout Rooms (In Person)

Breakout rooms were assigned verbally.

No one moved at first.

Eventually, everyone formed groups of four, spread across the room in loose circles of chairs.

"So," a person in one group said sarcastically, "I think the key takeaway here… professional boundaries."

"Yes," another smiled and agreed quickly. "Strong boundaries."

A third nodded. "Yup, boundaries."

No one elaborated.

Once the group settled on the established message, the discussion moved to gossip about the other attendees in the room.

Across the room, Alex and Jordan were placed in different groups by the trainer. Neither spoke.

This was either intentional or an accident that would be discussed later.

They looked somewhat relieved, but hesitant, also unsure if the separation was intentional.

The intern fixed a fake microphone issue, then stood very still, unsure where to stand that did not make things worse.

10:15 AM — Elsewhere, Work Continues

While Finance and Operations discussed hypotheticals and increasing awkward situations, the rest of the company worked.

In **Payments War Room - Lite**, Sam watched metrics settle into an uneasy calm.

From the podium in the training room, the intern glanced at the dashboards on his second laptop from the training room between slide transitions.

Green held.

10:30 AM – Marketing Momentum

In **Marketing**, Derrick joined a separate call titled:

Feature Momentum Sync

This one had an agenda, since it was Derrick's meeting for his team's work.

"We need a win," Derrick said immediately. "Something forward-looking."

Thad joined briefly, audio only.

"It's not stable yet," Thad said. "We're in process of pushing a hotfix."

Derrick nodded sympathetically. "Totally. But from a narrative standpoint?"

Thad disconnected.

Derrick turned to Tom, his Director of Product & Branding.

"Let's draft language that's aspirational but flexible."

Tom opened a new document and started drafting:

— — —

[Document]

Launch Messaging (Draft 1)

Overview

Today marks another step forward in our continued evolution of the payments platform. As customer needs grow and usage patterns shift, we remain focused on delivering resilient, scalable solutions that support long-term momentum.

What's New

- Ongoing enhancements to platform performance and responsiveness
- Continued investment in infrastructure designed to support peak demand
- Incremental improvements informed by real-world usage

What This Means for Customers

Customers may notice improved consistency during high-volume periods, reflecting our commitment to learning, adapting, and strengthening the platform over time.

Positioning Guidance

- Emphasize momentum, not milestones
- Avoid references to specific performance metrics
- Frame changes as part of a broader modernization journey
- Reinforce stability as an outcome, not a promise

Suggested Language

"We're excited about the progress underway as we continue building a more resilient payments experience. Every improvement helps us better support our customers today and as we grow together."

— — —

11:15 AM — The Video Attendees Speak

Back in the training session, Emily chimed back in.

"Just want to say," they said, smiling with the careful neutrality of someone who had been coached, "we really appreciate everyone being flexible today."

Flexible was a stretch.

In the back of the room, Alex and Jordan sat very still, in a way that suggested they had recently learned the human body could, in fact, lock itself. They were now sitting 2 chairs apart.

Jessica nodded from the back of the room, where no one on screen could see her. She waited a beat, just long enough for the silence to notice itself, then spoke.

"I realize this is uncomfortable," she said gently, with the voice she used for layoffs and bereavement cards. "But growth often is." She made sure not to look down at the two seated in front of her in the back row.

Someone in the third row snickered, immediately regretted it, and compensated by coughing too hard. Another chair squeaked. No one made eye contact with anyone else, but several people stared directly at the carpet, as if answers might be down there.

At the front of the room, the intern advanced the slide again.

Relationships at Work

The title was abstract. The examples provided were not.

The facilitator leaned forward slightly, adopting the posture of someone about to read from a script they hadn't written but would be blamed for anyway.

"Power dynamics," they said, carefully, "don't require a formal reporting relationship to exist."

A pause.

"Or," they added, "for both parties to agree on what's happening."

Several cameras on the screen went dark at once, like a power outage that had decided to be selective.

Alex shifted again, this time too late to pretend it was casual.

Jessica nodded thoughtfully, pretending as if considering the concept for the first time.

"This is really about protecting everyone involved," she said. "Including the broader team."

No one asked who *everyone* was.

No one asked who the broader team was protecting themselves *from*.

The intern advanced the slide.

Examples (Hypothetical)

The word *hypothetical* appeared in parentheses, as though that settled something.

The facilitator read the first bullet aloud.

"An employee with informal influence engages in repeated inappropriate or personal interactions with a colleague at the individual contributor level during or outside of work hours."

The facilitator looked up. Smiled reassuringly. Then continued reading the provided script.

"This could include," they continued, "messages, jokes, or offers of private mentorship that may be perceived differently by each party."

Someone in the back row mouthed *oh no* without sound as they covered their mouth to prevent any lip reading.

Jessica folded her hands.

"And just to clarify," she said, still gentle, "we are not intending to tell adults how to live their lives, but perception is reality, and can be impacted very easily."

The slide did not move.

The facilitator did not elaborate.

Alex and Jordan stared straight ahead, as if eye contact with the screen might count as admission. Everyone else was either typing feverishly on their phones, or processing what just happened.

Finally, mercifully, the intern advanced the slide.

Anonymous Pulse Check

A soft chime sounded. On screen, a bar graph appeared, rendered in calming blues.

The facilitator smiled, the way people do when they believe data is neutral.

"We're going to do a quick, anonymous poll," they said. "Just to gauge how this is landing."

A QR code appeared.

Phones came out instantly. Many were already in hand, finishing up the stream of gossip amongst themselves. No one looked at anyone else.

The question faded in beneath the graph:

Have you ever felt uncomfortable due to a colleague's behavior at work?

The bars began to move almost as fast as the bodies shifted in chairs.

Yes — 72%

Not sure — 23%

No — 5%

Once results posted, you could hear a pin drop. No one dared make eye contact, to prevent acknowledgement of the truth, or prevent admitting guilt.

The facilitator nodded, as if this were reassuring.

"That's very common," they said quickly. "And exactly why these conversations matter."

In the back row, Jordan was thinking about crossing his arms. Alex uncrossed hers, then recrossed them, choosing a different configuration.

Jessica tilted her head, studying the screen.

"What's important," she said to the room, "is that discomfort often goes unspoken until moments like this."

The intern did not advance the slide.

The next question appeared automatically.

Have you ever worried that reporting a concern might negatively affect your career?

The bars moved faster this time.

Yes — 81%

Someone let out a short, involuntary laugh. It died alone.

On screen, Jessica's face froze for half a second before resuming its attentive neutrality.

"Well," Emily said, unhelpfully, "that's… good insight."

No one wrote that down.

Jessica clasped her hands.

"This is why we emphasize psychological safety," she said, gently, firmly, as if speaking to a skittish animal. "And why we encourage early conversations."

Alex and Jordan, at the center of the current universe, stared straight ahead. Their normally perfectly tanned skin looking a very pale hue, mixed with blotched, red patches. Neither blinked.

The intern advanced the slide.

Questions & Discussion

A collective, silent *oh God* passed through the room.

The facilitator brightened.

"This is an opportunity," they said, "to ask anything you're unsure about."

No one raised a hand. Some prayed that they would not be called on.

Seconds stretched into what felt like months.

On screen, someone's microphone clicked on.

It was a junior analyst. No one knew their name. This would not help.

"Hi," they said, voice thin but determined. "I just wanted to clarify—if something feels ambiguous, but there's no explicit request, is that still something HR would want to know about?"

The room stopped breathing.

The facilitator nodded slowly.

"Yes," they said. "Ambiguity is often where issues begin."

Jessica leaned forward.

"And to add," she said, "patterns matter."

She paused.

"Even when individual moments seem small."

The analyst nodded, having already begun to regret everything.

Someone raised their hand in the room.

Someone more confident. It was Rachel.

"So," they said, "what if the behavior is consensual, but later becomes uncomfortable for them or everyone around them?"

Jessica didn't hesitate.

"Consent can change," she said. "Power dynamics don't always."

No one moved.

No one breathed.

The facilitator glanced at the clock.

"We have time for one more question."

A hand went up in the room.

Everyone turned.

It was Alex.

She cleared her throat and paused. Her face was snow white at this point.

"I just want to understand," they said, voice carefully level, "how to avoid… misinterpretation." She was not looking for an answer, but making a statement out loud as if blaming the group for misinterpreting the situation.

They were not misinterpreting.

The facilitator smiled, relieved. This was a question they could answer.

"Great question," they said. "The safest approach is to keep interactions professional, documented, and observable."

Jessica nodded once.

"And when in doubt," she added, "err on the side of less."

Silence followed. Awkward, but educational, silence.

The intern advanced the slide.

Key Takeaways

No one read them.

The training would continue after a working lunch break.

Two people were learning a lot.

Everyone else learned nothing new.

12:50 PM — Lunch (Still Not Lunch)

Since it was a training class—and at least one executive was in the room, lunch was catered.

It was from Tony's.

Tony's was a local sandwich shop that Tina used for **every** working lunch. No one knew why. It could have been the cheap prices. It could have been reliability and on-time delivery. It could have been that Tina was Tony's sister.

Either way, the food arrived exactly as it always did.

The hoagies were technically sandwiches, in the sense that they met the legal definition. The bread was stale enough to resist compression, forcing everyone to open their mouths wider than necessary, like snakes swallowing prey. Inside, mayonnaise was lathered on too heavy, distributed unevenly, as if applied by someone had never made a sandwich before. There was one thin slice of ham. One thin slice of cheese. They did not overlap. Between them sat a single, shriveled pickle slice, clinging to life. If you were lucky, there were two.

The sides were worse.

Each meal came with a small bag of generic brand potato chips, containing exactly five chips and a lot of air, but yet all still somehow broken. Dessert was either a chocolate chip cookie that appeared to be made from recycled office furniture or a brownie-flavored brick. Biting into either produced no crumbs, only sadness and jaw pain. The facilitator distributed small water bottles to wash down the shrapnel that would stick to everyone's throats.

People ate quietly.

Except those that bit down too fast on the dessert and hurt themselves.

Chewing was slow and deliberate, the way it is when dental insurance has known limits. Plates were balanced on notepads. Napkins were deployed strategically, less for cleanliness and more for spitting food into and discreetly discarding. Someone attempted to unwrap their sandwich and stopped halfway, reconsidering their life choices.

Alex and Jordan did not sit together.

They sat with their respective teams, on opposite sides of the room, angled away from one another in a manner that felt intentional but not rehearsed. Both pretended to be deeply engaged in work-related conversation that no one was really listening to, nodding at appropriate intervals, laughing a half-second too late. They avoided eye contact with one another.

Occasionally, they both looked up at the same time.

Not at each other.

At the intern.

Their eyes met there for a brief second, then snapped away, as if contact through a third party still counted.

The intern, sensing this, crouched down and began troubleshooting a cable that did not need troubleshooting. The cable was firmly connected. It had always been firmly connected. The intern unplugged it anyway, stared at it thoughtfully, then plugged it back in, hoping the problem, whatever it was, would resolve itself.

Lunch continued.

No one finished their food.

Everyone pretended they had.

The trach can overflowed.

2:00 PM — Training Continues (Somehow)

Attendance remained high, though participation waned.

In the background, Jackie and his minions entered at a pre-determined time and worked with Tina to collect the untouched food to send to the breakroom for anyone to pick up that wanted something. It would sit there for a few days prior to being tossed.

It would not mold nor become any more stale in those few days.

During class, someone answered every poll with *Strongly Agree* without reading the question.

The facilitator called this engagement.

Jessica called it progress.

At 2:37 PM, Facilities sent another email.

— — —

[Email]
From: Facilities
Subject: Reminder - Food
All,

Facilities would like to thank everyone for participating in today's training session.

As a follow-up, we observed a higher-than-usual volume of uneaten catered food following lunch. While we understand that schedules and appetites may vary, we want to take a moment to remind teams of our shared responsibility to minimize food waste.

To support this effort, please consider the following best practices for future sessions:

- Only take food you intend to consume
- Communicate dietary preferences in advance when possible

- Notify Facilities if catering quantities should be adjusted

Reducing waste helps us remain cost-conscious and environmentally responsible.

Thank you for your cooperation.

- Jackie
Facilities Operations & Workplace Services

— — —

The email was followed immediately by a Teams notification to the entire company.

— — —

[Teams | Company Announcements]

Facilities (3:45 PM)
Reminder: Please adhere to room reservation guidelines and vacate shared spaces promptly after meetings. Rooms found to be unoccupied during scheduled reservations may be released and made available without notice. Facilities personnel will be conducting routine walk-throughs to ensure compliance.

— — —

The intern saw the email and Teams notification pop up on training screen and minimized both quickly. They knew it was not related to any extracurricular activities since anyone normally involved in said activities was currently in the training class. Unless there were more?

The afternoon section covered **Trust and Accountability**.

The facilitator asked for volunteers to read scenarios aloud.

No one volunteered.

Jessica smiled encouragingly from the screen.

"Remember," she said, "this is a safe space."

No one felt unsafe. More sleepy at this point.

Participants were then "volun-told," since there were no hands raised.

The intern advanced slides, avoided eye contact, and became deeply aware of how visible a person becomes when they are not the subject of a meeting but cannot leave it.

3:15 PM — Marketing Needs a Win

By the fourth draft, the marketing product feature announcement no longer resembled anything that had actually happened.

Derrick scrolled through it once, then again, nodding as if the words were reporting progress back to him personally. The language had been cleaned. Smoothed. Filed down until it could no longer catch on anything sharp.

"Early preview."

"Limited rollout."

"Demonstrating momentum."

Every phrase had survived Legal. That alone felt like success.

There were no dates. No numbers. No references to performance, stability, or outcomes that could later be interpreted as promises. Even the word *launch* had been quietly replaced with *phase*, which Derrick agreed sounded both intentional and reversible.

Tom watched him read, hands folded, waiting.

"This is good," Derrick said finally. "This is safe."

Tom nodded, though his expression suggested the kind of safety usually associated with guardrails and padded rooms.

"So," Tom said carefully, "are we sure this won't conflict with the incident?"

Derrick looked up.

"What incident?" he asked, genuinely.

Tom blinked. Once.

"The payments latency," he said. "The war room. The alerts. Thad—"

Derrick waved a hand, already smiling.

"That's not an incident," he said. "That's context."

He tapped the screen.

"This," he added, "is narrative."

Tom glanced back at the document. At the careful absence of specifics. At the sentence that said *customers may notice improved consistency*, which technically did not promise anything, least of all improvement.

"And we're comfortable calling this an early preview?" Tom asked.

Derrick nodded again, more firmly this time.

"It's aspirational," he said. "But flexible."

Tom made a note he would later delete.

Derrick signed off as *Approved.*

The document updated.

Somewhere else in the building, Thad was still waiting for alerts to turn yellow to reflect something close to reality.

Tom asked one question. "Are we sure this won't conflict with the incident?"

Derrick smiled. "What incident?"

Tom did not respond.

The document went out.

— — —

[Document]
Launch Messaging — Draft 4 (Legal Review Complete)

Overview

This communication is intended to reflect ongoing platform evolution in alignment with broader strategic initiatives.

What's Included

- An early preview of potential capabilities
- A limited rollout framework
- Indicators of forward momentum

Important Clarification

This messaging does not constitute a commitment, guarantee, representation, or assurance regarding functionality, availability, performance, timelines, outcomes, or customer experience.

Notes

All language has been reviewed for consistency with applicable guidance.

———

3:47 PM – Engineering Sees It

———

[Teams | Engineering]

Ortega, Sam (3:47 PM)
Is this about the thing that's still on fire that may not even be related?

Chen, Maya (3:48 PM)
"Does not constitute" is doing a lot of work here.

Natarajan, Priya (3:48 PM)
I will save a copy.

Brooks, Evan (3:49 PM)
Do we need to answer questions about this?

Reynolds, Thad (3:50 PM)
No. We have yet to figure out why this isn't showing in monitors, or how to tie it back to the actual root cause.

— Chen, Maya reacted with 👍 —
— Ortega, Sam reacted with 👍 —

— — —

The Intern read the messages and said nothing.

4:30 PM — Training Wrap-Up

The final slide appeared.

Thank You for Your Commitment to Excellence

Jessica returned to the front of the room and stood next to Emily.

"I know this was a long day," she said. "But these conversations matter."

No one disagreed. One or two raised their heads from the table, waking from their impromptu naps.

"If anyone has questions," Emily stated, "please reach out to HR."

"You can also schedule something with me directly," Jessica added.

Her calendar was full for the next three weeks.

Polite applause followed. Not synchronized.

The class ended. The senior leadership that joined remotely had been off camera by early afternoon, and their profile pictures stayed in the session and muted until the intern disconnected everyone that was left.

A few people gathered their things quickly and left. This was the only meeting on their calendar for the day, so it was taken as an early release pass. The rest lingered in the room so that they wouldn't have to go back to the real world for the last 30-60 minutes of the day, and could then quietly clock out and disappear to the parking lot or private huddle rooms.

Jessica and Emily thanked the intern and left, leaving the cleanup to be handled alone. The intern packed up the laptop, coiled the cables carefully, and noticed that the room felt lighter now that no one was pretending anything anymore. At 4:45 PM, Jackie poked his head in the door.

"Thad said you guys finished already? Need help getting everything cleaned out? I can get my guys down here quick to reset the room. Thad says you're good people."

"I'm ok, just packing up the last few things now, and you can have the room back, but thank you," the intern responded.

Outside, work continued. There was still IT work to do prior to leaving for the day.

6:15 PM — IT Stays Late

By 5:00 PM, the intern had finished cleaning up, and returned fully to work. Jackie's minions had the room fully reset by 5:05 PM, as they were waiting outside the door for the intern to exit so that they could swarm in and finish up.

The systems were stable.

The workaround remained in place.

Luis' hotfix was being peer reviewed by Thad.

At 6:15 PM, A new Jira ticket appeared, preparing for the code push.

— — —

[Work Item]

Title: Review Sandbox Deployment Controls
Priority: Medium
Owner: TBD

— — —

The intern was not assigned.

They closed their laptop carefully.

Tomorrow, there would be process.

Tonight, there was only monitoring.

But while observing, the intern watched a quiet pattern emerge.

Retries hadn't returned.

Latency was acceptable.

The Intern refreshed the page.

Their system access still worked.

For now.

WEDNESDAY: "Visibility & Transparency"

Mostly neither.

8:25 AM — The All-Hands

Attendance was the highest it had been all quarter.

Executive leadership was on-site in the auditorium. Those in-office were in attendance in the large space. Anyone outside the headquarters would join via web.

Cameras on: twelve.

Cameras off: everyone else.

Once the virtual attendees realized the meeting was visible to the auditorium, they switch off cameras quickly. Not before the crowd took note of everyone attending from home, in their pajamas, not being forced to work in-office.

Eugene and William sat side-by-side in the center of the small stage, with executives lined on each side. From left to right they sat: Barbara, Jessica, Bob, Eugene, William, Declan, Karen, and Derrick. Thad stayed at the back of the auditorium in the sound booth with his team. He rarely had speaking parts in these all-hands, since nothing he would have to say related to revenue generation, partnership opportunities, or expense reduction. The executives' attire was respectively the same as always. Their clothing costing more than some employees made in a month.

The marketing team had a content manager, Lily, that also doubled as a part-time makeup artist, hair stylist, and photographer, always ready to make sure the team looked good for video during events like these. She was an influencer outside of work that made social media makeup tutorials, and had gathered a pretty impressive following. Some of the team needed more work than others. Bob particularly had to have product put in his hair to prevent the bad hair dye from running into his face and collar from the hot overhead lighting. Derrick's sunglasses had to be removed, leaving him making a constant squinting face the entire meeting.

Seeing Karen in person was an anomaly. The stories didn't do her justice. She barley looked five foot tall, about 3 inches of which were her red-bottomed, black high-heeled shoes. The red was a piercing contrast to the fitted, black on black pant suit. Her black hair was immaculate, and there wasn't a single wrinkle on her face, apparently because she hasn't smiled once in her life, or Botox had wiped out any resemblance of humanity.

William was the first to stand and move to the podium to the right of the exec lineup, as the large screen behind them switched from a "Welcome Team" graphic to the camera pointed on the podium. As he tapped the microphone, "Good morning, everyone," he said. "Really excited to see such strong attendance."

The video conference showed 4,102 participants online, with the auditorium holding at least another 500 more.

No one responded.

"Before we jump in," William continued, "I just want to acknowledge—it's been a challenging but exciting week."

This sentence had been workshopped.

The exec team nodded from their chairs like bobbleheads.

"Thank you, William," someone online said, which echoed through the auditorium.

Panic hit the support team in the booth, as the engineer jumped at the admin panel. The chat was immediately disabled and all mics muted by the AV Support team from the booth. Thad made an apologetic wave from the back to the exec team showing that they were all clear to continue.

Anonymous Q&A was enabled.

The first slide appeared behind Eugene:

THIS WEEK: CHALLENGES & OPPORTUNITIES

It was Wednesday.

"We've seen incredible resilience across teams," William said. "A lot of great collaboration. A lot of alignment."

Thad watched his laptop from the booth. Teams open.

In **Payments War Room - Lite**, the workaround was still holding. The hotfix would be pushed later that day. His development and engineering teams team stayed at their desk in network operations center to continue monitoring, while halfway listening to the all-hands call.

From **Marketing**, Derrick had assigned Tom to jot down any good phrases made by exec that he could reuse later.

William continued, "As you may know by now, the board of directors will be visiting tomorrow. The executive team has done a tremendous amount of work preparing for their arrival. I hope that we all come to work tomorrow dressed for success, to show our parent company that we are a solid group of professionals here for a unified purpose."

As he continued to prep the audience for the content to be discussed, he looked down at the laptop on the podium that IT had setup in order for the Q&A chat to be visible to the presentable.

8:35 AM — The Question

The first anonymous question appeared.

Anonymous: Are layoffs planned?

The question sat there.

Long enough to be read.

Long enough to be reread.

Long enough for people watching the chat to start wondering who had typed it and whether they were still employed.

William smiled gently.

"There is a question in the chat about potential layoffs. That's a great question," he said.

He paused, the way people pause when choosing language that cannot be misquoted because it contains nothing.

"What I'll say," William continued, "is that we're always evaluating how to best position the company for long-term success."

Jessica leaned forward slightly.

Declan nodded ferociously in agreement.

"And we're committed to doing that with empathy and transparency," she added.

No one knew what that meant.

The question remained unanswered.

Another similar anonymous question appeared.

It was not addressed.

"Let's welcome Bob up to talk about everyone's favorite topic, Finance & Accounting."

8:50 AM — Selective Transparency

Bob took a deep breath and swayed back, then forward, in order to give himself enough inertia to get out of the chair with a loud grunt. He slowly made his way to the podium. His hair dye was holding strong, as the makeup artist performed masterful work keeping the spiderweb thin hair in check.

"Thanks, Bill." He stated. William did not like being called Bill. He was a native of the UK, and any nicknames such as Bill, Billy, King William, and others that had been stated in meetings or chats, whether in passing or as a joke, all sat poorly with him. He had made this known to a few that had tried it in the past, but Bob had never tried prior to this very public display, so he could only nod with a noticeable grimace on his face, and take his seat back in the center of the stage.

"From a financial standpoint," he said, almost as if out of breath from the short walk from the side of the stage, "we remain dynamic."

This was not elaborated on. He quickly went through a few additional slides on the P&L, EBITDA, and a few other acronym that only execs and finance types care about. The audience sat glazed, or on their phones. He then called out Derrick to speak next and slowly waddled back to his seat.

Derrick spoke next. He had a relaxed strut to the podium, choosing the brightest of pink quarter-zips to go with this Navy checkered blazer. This combination, along with sky blue slacks, white belt, and white athletic dress shoes, made the halo on the camera unavoidable. The engineers turned the lighting down on stage a bit to try to help. Derrick looked like he was about to play 18 as soon as this meeting was over. He just needed to ditch the jacket.

"From a brand and product perspective," he said, "momentum is strong. We have a new product feature set hitting next week for soft launch, and our clients are excited to get started using them. We will be streamlining a few processes, automating a lot of what were previous manual pain points, and refreshing the UI to be cleaner for all that use it. In the next quarter or so, we will also be evaluating the use of AI through a few streams, to include chat, payment verification, and automated reconciliation." A slide sat on the screen showing icons, flows, and timelines for features that Thad nor his team had any knowledge of.

Thad's heart jumped into his throat, as he turned to his a few of his developers that were sitting in the back next to the booth and silently mouthed, "What the #$%^ is he talking about??" The developers looked just as surprised as he did, and shrugged their shoulders, confirming that this was a vaporware slide that everyone is seeing for the first time. The executives on the panel were nodding and making faces as if very impressed that this was on the horizon.

"With that exciting news in your pocket to keep the crowd awake, let's go back to other news: Operations. Dex, come on up." He winked as Declan grimaced at the nickname that no one was allowed to use.

Instead of strolling back to his seat, Derrick exited stage right, and headed toward the exit, removing his blazer at the same time. His tee time with a potential new client was in 45 minutes. He couldn't be late.

Declan walked to the podium with intent. As he reached the podium, the slide advanced to:

OPERATIONAL RESILIENCE

No metrics were shown. Only a table that showed the number of headcount per office, both in-office and remote. He spoke on a few slides that were previously present by Bob as well as the positive impacts on expenses that the new product and features could have on the company, and operations specifically. The audience was now squirming their seats, as this sounded more like foreshadowing than it did a pep-talk about company growth.

"I'm sure you will all agree that the work we are doing is great for the organization. We will remove any inefficiencies, call out the process and people that are holding us back, and enforce positive growth in the year ahead," he said coldly, and with a demeanor that felt like he believe everyone was in agreement with him.

Execs made no movement or acknowledgement of the operations slide. Most of the panel looked down. William scanned the audience to measure response. Jessica looked straight ahead, making eye contact only with the small red light on the camera, not realizing it was currently pointed directly at her while panning across the leadership team. Her right eye began to noticeably twitch.

Thad looked down to check the Teams Q&A thread.

9:45 AM — The Question That Breaks the Room

Someone asked about system stability.

The wording was careful. It had likely been drafted offline.

Anonymous: Have there been any recent incidents affecting customers?

Declan said what he needed to say, and did not intend to answer any questions. He called up Eugene to take over, and sat back down.

Eugene walked up quietly, looked at the question on the podium laptop, and nodded thoughtfully.

"Thank you, Declan. I see the question from the audience about system stability. I'm glad that was asked," he said. "It shows engagement."

This was not an answer.

"What I can share," he continued, "is that our systems are designed to handle stress."

The slide behind him changed. He was not aware a slide for systems made it into the deck. It was not there on the last pass he made prior to the all-hands meeting.

— — —

[Presentation Slide]

STRESS TESTS ARE PART OF GROWTH

What happened

- Elevated latency during peak demand window

Why it happened

- Live-traffic stress testing exceeded simulated load models

What it proved

- System recovered without data loss

- Degradation followed predicted patterns
- Bottleneck identified and isolated

What changes

- Capacity thresholds updated
- Queuing logic adjusted
- Alerting tuned to real-world behavior

Latency is a signal, not a failure.

— — —

No one on the exec team knew who had written that, but they could probably guess. Eugene couldn't question it from the podium, but he continued.

Jessica looked at Thad in the AV booth and smiled.

Thad shrugged as if he didn't know about it either.

At 10:00 AM, Jessica wrapped the meeting with a few culture talking points, and a simple "Thank you for joining us. We look forward to seeing you again at the next all-hands next quarter," as the executive team gave quick presidential waves as they exited the stage. No input from any of the other leaders, as they were only there to show strong leadership support for the message. They had become professionals at sitting for hours, saying nothing, and just being faces of the company for meetings like these.

11:30 AM — Legal Review Spiral

Karen scheduled a meeting.

It was titled **Messaging Alignment**.

It included Eugene, William, Declan, Tom, and Jessica. Derrick was already one drink in, and about to be on his second at the golf course. He would not risk it, and needed Tom to cover.

Thad was not invited.

The meeting produced a client announcement pertaining to the new product features being deployed within the next week, as well as lightly addressing the latency issues reported and displayed in the all-hands by the unknown assailant for the entire company to see. This would protect them if any client were to come to them as actually having latency issues that had not been previously reported.

The document removed:

- Specifics
- Timelines
- Ownership

What remained was tone.

The phrase *"intermittent latency"* was replaced with *"brief service interruption."*

The word *"cause"* was removed entirely.

Karen approved it. Jessica sent it out to through corporate communications. Tom added the document to the product release logs as a deployment artifact.

2:00 PM — Status Is Still Green

The dashboard was still green.

It had been green throughout the entire latency issue. That couldn't be right.

Maya updated the status anyway.

Status: Monitoring

No one questioned it.

Thad had his team research more anyway.

Sam and Evan delegated.

"Make the intern do it."

The intern had been provided access to the monitors to check logic used to determine the status. The monitors were a third party system that simply aggregated logs from other systems and presented a screen of gauges based on the data and configured monitor settings. There was nothing custom about it. You setup a new data feed, choose the applicable alert levels, and present a gauge on the screen that moves from red to green accordingly. This shouldn't be a big task to triage.

All of the above was correct:

- The endpoints were connected successfully.
- The alert was polling on a set schedule
- The data in the endpoint was formatted correctly.

But…

! Alert Type was still set to the default value of "Average Latency" instead of the needed p95 (95%) latency.

! The default alert polling was for 60 minutes instead of 60 seconds.

The intern checked his runbooks.

Then checked them again.

Then cross-referenced the configuration guide, the user documentation, and the section everyone skimmed.

Thirty-five minutes later, he opened Teams.

— — —

[Teams | Payments War Room – Lite]

Intern (2:35 PM)
Mr. Reynolds, I think I figured out why the monitor never turned yellow or red.

Reynolds, Thad (2:36 PM)
Oh yeah? That was fast. What've you got? And don't call me that.

Brooks, Evan (2:36 PM)
Yeah right.

Ortega, Sam (2:36 PM)
I checked the monitors twice. They were fine.

Intern (2:38 PM)
Um. Well, based on the documentation, we're still using the default polling configuration.
Polling is set to 60 minutes instead of 60 seconds.
And the latency check is set to 'Average Latency', not 'P95.'

— Brooks, Evan is typing… —
— Brooks, Evan stopped typing —

— Ortega, Sam is typing… —
— Ortega, Sam stopped typing —

Reynolds, Thad (2:40 PM)
C'mon, guys. Spit it out.
I can see you typing.
Did the intern just find something in thirty minutes that we didn't see for a couple of days?

Brooks, Evan (2:41 PM)
Yes.

Reynolds, Thad (2:41 PM)
Yes what?

Brooks, Evan (2:42 PM)
Yes, he figured it out.
Dammit.

Ortega, Sam (2:45 PM)
Good catch, Intern.
You beat us.

Intern (2:45 PM)
Sorry — I wasn't trying to call anyone out.

Reynolds, Thad (2:46 PM)
Oh no, don't mind them.
They deserve a good beating.
Keeps them humble.

Brooks, Evan (2:47 PM)
Shut your face, Thaddeus.

Ortega, Sam (2:47 PM)
I'm never living this down.

Reynolds, Thad (2:50PM)
You are correct, Samuel.
Alright, Intern.
Since you found the gap, you can fix it.

Evan and Sam will do the peer review so they can learn what it's supposed to look like.
I'll draft a summary in case leadership wants details.
I'm positive they'll understand everything we're saying here.
☺

Brooks, Evan (2:51 PM)
Ha. Nice.

— — —

By 3:45 PM, Thad had written a carefully translated summary explaining what had happened, why it wasn't caught sooner, and how no one should feel bad about it—
which ensured that several people immediately did.

— — —

[Email]

From: Reynolds, Thad
To: Executive Committee
Subject: Monitoring Alert Configuration – Latency Incident

Executive Committee,

Engineering has completed a review of why the monitoring platform did not flag the recent latency issue in real time.

We identified two configuration oversights in the alerting setup:

- Alerts were still polling system data every **60 minutes**, rather than the intended **60 seconds**, which caused short but meaningful latency spikes to be missed.

- Latency alerts were based on **average response time**, rather than **p95 (worst-case) response time**, which meant customer-impacting delays were masked by otherwise normal traffic.

As a result, the monitoring dashboard remained green and did not escalate to yellow, even though a subset of users was experiencing degraded performance.

Both settings have now been corrected. The dashboard is reflecting real-time conditions accurately, and alert thresholds are aligned to customer experience rather than system averages.

No data loss occurred. The issue was one of visibility, not system stability.

Please let me know if you'd like a brief walkthrough of the changes.

Thad Reynolds
Chief Technology Officer

— — —

Eugene, Delcan, and Karen gave a thumbs up reaction to the email in Outlook. No responses otherwise. Thad assumed that would be the reaction.

4:45 PM — Executive Reframing

Eugene sent an email to the company.

— — —

[Email]

From: Caldwell, Eugene
Subject: Momentum & Alignment

Team,

I want to thank everyone for the incredible focus and collaboration this week.

We experienced a brief stress test that demonstrated the resilience of our platform and the strength of our teams.

Proud of how aligned we are as we move forward!

More soon,
Eugene

— — —

Thad read it twice. He didn't know whether to laugh or be offended that the executive team basically dismissed his deck slide that they knew he added, and the supplemental information that he had sent based on the additional due diligence.

In **Payments War Room - Lite**, Sam and Evan reacted with thumbs up emoji when asked if anyone read Eugene's email.

The intern read it once and felt a strange sense of distance, like watching footage of an event they had attended but not recognized. Is this how most IT teams are treated at other companies?

5:00 PM — The Poker Game

At exactly 5:00 PM, while Eugene's email was still being forwarded with increasingly creative commentary, Thad opened Teams and changed the tone of the day.

He invited people to poker night.

The message appeared in **The Crew** channel—a channel the intern had not been a member of until three minutes earlier, when Thad quietly added him without comment.

— — —

[Teams | The Crew]

Reynolds, Thad (5:00 PM)
Monthly poker game this Friday at my place.
7:00 PM.
Casual.
Same rules as always.
As always — what happens at Thad's stays at Thad's.

— — —

Reactions appeared quickly.

Cards. Hearts. Spades. Jokers.

A poker chip.

An 👀 emoji appeared, then vanished.

This was apparently not new information. It was standard practice.

The intern stared at it longer than necessary.

Poker night had been mentioned before. Usually vague references, always after incidents, always in a way that suggested it was both optional and mandatory in the way trust-building often is. Sam and Evan were the most vocal about it in side conversations, but also cryptic. It felt like poker night was equivalent to a fight club.

The intern typed.

Deleted.

Typed again.

Intern (5:03 PM)
Just confirming… this is actual poker game, right?
Not a metaphor.
And you meant to invite me?

Three dots appeared.
Disappeared.
Reappeared.

Ortega, Sam (5:04 PM)
Very real.
Bring cash.
Don't bring work.

Brooks, Evan (5:04 PM)
Don't talk about work.
Especially alert monitors.
I will end you.

Several people reacted with 😂.

Chen, Maya (5:05 PM)
No logging, decks, or postmortems.
My sister will be coming in my stead.
I have a conflict I can't get out of.

Sam reacted with 🙏.

Thad replied once more.

Reynolds, Thad (5:06 PM)
There will be poker, beverages, and some food.
There will be others there from outside of IT as well.
Bring your spouse, partner, significant other, or any term you're comfortable with.
This is not an employee-only event.
It's simply a Cool-Person-Only event.
BYOB if you want something specific.
You cannot have any of my good scotch.
Well.
Maybe one shot.

— Brooks, Evan reacted with 😂 —

The intern hovered over the same reaction.

Added 👍.

Paused.

Left it.

For the first time all week, the message required no translation. But it was weird being invited to a executive leader's place for poker as an intern. It felt cool.

Thad closed Teams.

The systems were stable.

The monitors were monitoring accurately.

Friday had been acknowledged.

Hump Day was complete.

THURSDAY: "The Board Is Coming"

Panic with PowerPoint.

7:58 AM — The Deck Panic Begins

By Thursday, Tina had probably sent about 20 reminder emails about the board coming. She would walk the halls checking to make sure cubes were straight, ensuring that employees were dressed in at least business casual and looking busy. She paid special attention to one section of cubes in the marketing department everyone referred to as "Melrose Place."

This was the home base for a group of woman that were more silicone and makeup than human. They liked to get as close to violating dress code policies as they could on a daily basis. They were loud, gossipy, and colorful. They either married money and had the job to keep from being bored, or they were looking for an exec to marry and not have to work anymore.

They reported to Lily, the Content Manager, spending their days discussing the latest fashion trends, creating superficial social media content for the company, discussing their new fad diets or "gym fits." Their volume increased as senior leadership passed by the area, hoping to catch their attention. Lily kept Jessica on speed dial because of the women on her team.

At 7:58 AM, Thad noticed that the calendar invite titled **Board Touchpoint** had expanded from thirty minutes to two hours and now included three people whose titles contained the word *Partner.*

That was how it started.

Teams messages multiplied quickly.

"Is this the *full* board?"

"Do we know what they're focused on?"

"Has anyone seen the latest numbers?"

By 8:04 AM, the phrase *"we need to finish that deck"* had been typed six times by four different people.

By 8:07 AM, Bob's team was already rebuilding forecasts that had been finalized Tuesday night.

By 8:10 AM, Rachel was on her third version.

No one asked what changed.

8:32 AM — Emergency Deck Updates

Slides appeared rapidly in shared folders with names like:

- **Board_vFINAL**
- **Board_vFINAL_REAL**
- **Board_vFINAL_USE_THIS_ONE**

Fonts varied. Charts contradicted each other. Colors suggested urgency without specifying cause.

Declan joined a finance working session and immediately asked for headcount trends.

"Up or down?" he asked.

"Stable," Rachel said.

Bob frowned. "Declan, we'll show discipline, but not make this look like a RIF deck."

The numbers moved.

No one commented.

In Marketing, Derrick added a slide titled:

Momentum Highlights

It contained three bullets, none of which were technically complete, but the fonts "popped." He wasn't worried, because Tom would fix it. Derrick know that Tom knew what he meant to say.

Tom did not.

9:15 AM — Pre-Board Alignment

The pre-board meeting at 9 began fifteen minutes late and focused on ensuring William and Eugene had their final story straight.

Eugene spoke first.

"The goal today," he said, "is to tell a clear, aligned story."

William nodded in agreement.

Karen nodded. "Clarity is important," she said. "But so is caution."

Jessica smiled. "And empathy."

Derrick asked if the demo could still happen.

Thad was present but not invited to speak. He nodded to Derrick. Derrick smiled. That was all he really cared about.

When Thad did speak, it was to answer a question no one had asked.

"The systems are stable now, if anyone cares," he said.

Eugene nodded. "Great. Let's not over-index on technical detail."

Thad sighed and stopped talking.

11:00 AM — Unscheduled Grounds Maintenance

At 11:00 AM, while the board deck was being further refined for tone and survivability, Security and Facilities noticed something unusual happening on the front lawn.

The front lawn was being destroyed.

On a security monitors inside the Security Office, one of Jackie's minions was chatting with the security guard on duty, and watched as a large, black, lifted pickup truck breach the curb, accelerate onto the company's carefully landscaped green space, and begin carving confident, circular patterns into the grass. Beer cans flew from the driver side window while rebel yells filled the air.

"Uh. WTF is happening?" The guard exclaimed as he picked up the phone to call authorities.

The minion leaned around the guard and zoomed the camera in on the truck, following the driver through bushes and lawn ornaments like an NFL camera following the receiver running though the opposing defense.

After a full 15 minutes of lawn carnage, the truck stopped directly in front of the main entrance, as if he were ready to drive into the lobby itself. The driver revved the engine, causing a cloud of black smoke to encase the monster truck. The speakers blasted some form of death metal that rattled the windows of the truck and the lobby.

On-screen telemetry labeled the camera feed:

FRONT CAMPUS — CAMERA 3

The guard did not recognize the driver.

But he recognized the drunken body language.

11:04 AM — Identification

Jackie joined the group in the lobby.

"Oh, @#?!," he exclaimed. "That's Derrick!"

A pause. The minion looked confused.

"Not our Derrick," he clarified. "The other one. Donnelly."

That narrowed it slightly.

"Finance Director's husband," Jackie slowly added. "He goes by Double-D. No one here calls him that"

We will call him Double-D.

"Ooooohhh lawd geezus…" the guard exclaimed, wide eyed, apparently aware of the gossip involving Alex and Jordan.

The truck engine stopped.

The door of the massive 4x4 swung open again.

Double-D stepped out, unsteady but purposeful, scanning the building like it owed him something.

Detroit-born, but dressed like that geography was irrelevant, he moved with the swagger of someone who had learned masculinity from dirt tracks, trailer parks, and cable television. He wore a sleeveless black Pantera T-shirt that had once been a normal shirt, the armholes torn wide enough to make a point. Skinny, but wiry—muscle where it counted, the kind built from lifting things that didn't need lifting. He looked like he ran entirely on caffeine, nicotine, and unresolved grudges.

His skin was aggressively tan, the color of someone who believed sunscreen was created as part of a government conspiracy. A backward black ball cap was pulled tight over his head, as if to hold the mullet at bay. Tight jeans, worn thin at the knees, completed the look: functional, defiant, and a decade behind.

The mustache was the centerpiece. A full handlebar, waxed and deliberate, curling at the ends with the confidence of a man who had practiced in the mirror. The facial hair that screamed, "I don't drink no girly lite beer."

The anger sat on him like a second outfit. This was a man on fire. Outraged by betrayal. He was however, in every visible way, the last person you would expect Alex Donnelly to be married to.

Which somehow made him standing there, furious and very sure he was right, even more unsettling.

He shouted at the building as if it could hear him.

"JORDAN! YOU'RE DEAD! GET OUT HERE!".

He shouted it again, louder, with additional color.

The minion muted the feed instinctively, then unmuted it. Double-D was screaming things that would make a sailor blush.

11:17 AM — Alex Enters the Frame

A side door opened.

Then Alex walked into the frame.

"Oh, damn. Alex is out there now," Jackie stated.

She didn't run. She didn't even seemed to be in a hurry. She looked like someone who has dealt with this behavior before had already decided which version of this moment she would survive.

The two did not match. One could almost understand why she was fooling around with Jordan. They actually looked like a couple.

She walked slowly towards Double-D, showing little emotion, as if she was already done with the conversation before it started.

Double-D shouted again, but was mumbled and somewhat incoherent. Alex looked around at the damage he had caused.

Twin tire tracks carved deep into the grass, starting at the curb and ending nowhere in particular, as if the truck had entered with a plan and abandoned it halfway through. The sod was peeled back in long, angry strips, clumps of earth thrown aside like they'd been personally offensive. Where green had been, there was now a churned mixture of mud, clay, roots, and the unmistakable smell of overheated rubber.

Near the center, the damage tightened into tight, deliberate circles, executed slowly and with commitment. The grass there hadn't just been flattened; it had been erased. All that remained was a bald patch of compacted dirt, stamped with overlapping tread patterns, each one pressed in deeper than necessary, as if he'd gone around one more time just to be sure it hurt.

A decorative stone edging hadn't survived. Several of the rocks had been pushed out of place, one cracked clean in half, another embedded halfway into the lawn at an angle that suggested it had tried, unsuccessfully, to stand its ground. The small ornamental tree near the sign listing the company's values leaned noticeably to the left now, roots exposed, soil loosened as if it were considering leaving altogether.

The sign itself—*Integrity. Innovation. Trust.*—was splattered with mud up to waist height.

Closer to the building, the tracks swerved sharply, cutting across the lawn in a final, aggressive exit, having clipped a sprinkler head in the process. Water sprayed uselessly into the air, arcing over the destruction like a decorative finish.

Inside the building, windows were now lined with employees that wished they had a popcorn maker. This was the most excitement some of them had witnessed since starting their jobs at the company.

11:20 AM — Containment Fails

Alex said something the microphones did not pick up.

Double-D responded by gesturing broadly at the building, the lawn, and the general concept of betrayal.

Someone in finance whispered, "Should we call—"

The sirens answered first.

Two police cars entered the frame with professional boredom.

Double-D did not resist. He was ready.

He argued with Alex as he was walked away to the patrol car.

This felt consistent.

Alex stood still as he was guided away, the lawn behind her looking like an abstract painting of greens and browns.

The intern watched from the window. He watched the onlookers, realizing that they were more excited for the show than shocked that it happened. The only question in the intern's mind, "Is this a normal thing here?"

11:29 AM — Back Inside

Alex re-entered the building through a different door after talking to the police and thanking them for their help.

She did not look at the cameras.

She did not make eye contact with anyone.

She was mortified.

She walked directly into Bob's office who had just sat back down from the show.

"Alex," he said.

She waited.

"Have a seat. We need to talk," Bob said, already opening his laptop to take notes needed for an upcoming email to HR.

By 11:40 AM, Alex was no longer on any calendar invites.

By 11:45 AM, an HR placeholder appeared on Jessica's calendar.

Subject: Temporary Leave — Finance

Status: Pending Review

Jessica stared at it longer than necessary. She knew it was coming. She was in the lobby for the last half of the show as well. A few strands of hair fell from her manicured bun and into her face, as both eyes twitched now.

11:45 AM — Jessica, Briefly Unmasked

Jessica joined the call with Bob from her office. She did not feel up to an in-person conversation about what just transpired.

Her background was wrong. It was a generic beach scene she didn't remember selecting, the horizon slightly crooked, as if even the ocean had given up on alignment. Her smile arrived late—technically present, but clearly running behind schedule.

Bob spoke. Jessica listened. Or at least her face did.

"Yes," she said. "I'm aware."

Pause.

"Yes, unpaid for now. Few weeks"

Another pause.

"No," she said, evenly. "This is not disciplinary. This is procedural."

She pinched the bridge of her nose, then immediately stopped, aware—too late—that the gesture had been visible. She replaced it with a smile so quick and polished it almost passed for intentional.

"We'll sort it out," she said. "**We always do**."

She ended the call before Bob could say anything else.

For several seconds, she did not move.

Then her left eye twitched.

Just once.

Then again.

This was the third situation like this already this year, and it was only June.

She stared at her screen, at her own reflection now that the call had ended, and felt the familiar pressure build behind her eyes—the urge to scream, fully formed and articulate, like a sentence she'd been rehearsing for months. She didn't scream. She never did. Instead, she inhaled slowly, the way she'd taught herself to do after the second incident and before the first migraine.

Alex and Jordan had been testing her patience with the affair for a while now.

Not because anyone told her. Because the grapevine was loud. It always was. Because humans were terrible at secrets and excellent at repetition. She avoided documenting anything to avoid more accountability for yet another team member's stupidity. Just observations. Nothing actionable. Keeping only a mental folder labeled *Potentially Relevant.*

Her eye twitched again.

She stood up, paced once, then stopped, hands clenched at her sides, realizing she had reached the exact limit of her patience. Not crossed it. Reached it. The place where professionalism stopped being a virtue and started being blockage for expressing her frustration.

Jessica smoothed her blouse. Straightened her posture. Took one more deep breath. She slowly picked up a decorative pillow from her chair, place it gently over her face, and screamed as loud as she could. She sat the pillow back down, patting it back into its precise location on the chair.

She slowly opened her door, and went for a walk. There was a popular spot on the riverwalk behind the office building where many would spend their lunch hour sitting on the rocks, overlooking the small rapids, to forget the real world for a brief moment. Jessica visited this spot a lot.

11:55 AM — Narrative Containment

Facilities sent an email.

— — —

[Email]

From: Facilities
Subject: Grounds Maintenance Update

Please avoid the front lawn for the remainder of the day as we address unexpected, non-employee related landscaping damage.

- Jackie

— — —

Marketing did not respond.

Legal did not reply.

The board would never ask about the lawn, since the board room is on the back of the building facing the river, and would be guided in and out of the building through a different side entrance to avoid the scene of the crime.

The lawn would be replaced in the coming weeks.

Alex would not return for at least six weeks to let the story die down, to reduce any public appearance damage. Alex was fortunately very talented in her role in finance, and was one of Bob's favorites, so her long-term role was safe.

Jordan's calendar emptied itself for an equivalent number of weeks, but would end abruptly about two weeks in, as additional incidents related to other coworkers in "Melrose Place" started to surface while he was away. Apparently, multiple girls in the department were aware of Jordan's girlfriend, but not aware of Alex or each other. This odd spiderweb of jealously ensured the hole Jordan dug for himself was deep enough to fully bury him.

He would learn no lessons from this.

At noon, the board would be told the company was operating efficiently under pressure.

Which was technically true.

On the bright side, the board deck was progressing well.

12:00 PM — Selective Preparation

By late morning, the deck had become less accurate and more defensible.

Risk language was softened.

Timelines were abstracted.

The word *incident* was removed entirely.

Karen approved the final wording.

"This is safe," she said.

No one asked whether it was useful.

The intern was called in to load the deck to a presenter laptop, and prep the board room for the meeting. When the time came, they would stay along the back wall to assist as technical support in case anything happened with the presentation or equipment.

1:00 PM — Private Equity Arrives

The visitors arrived early, entering through the executive door form the parking garage, and moved directly into an open collaboration space in the side of the building.

They wore confidence like outerwear—tailored, layered, and difficult to remove.

The chairman of the parent private equity firm, M&A Capital, Inc, Robert DuFray, led them.

He was in his early sixties and dressed immaculately, the kind of immaculate that suggested planning and help from a second party. His custom tailored suit was bold navy with light gray pin stripes, sharply pressed, paired with a yellow patterned "power tie" that announced authority without asking permission. His shirt was starched to the point of hostility.

But his hair, though. It was… Different.

The toupee sat on his head like a bad decision that had been made years ago and now required constant defense. It barely covered the entire bald spot and was darker than the hair on the sides and back. It was shaped too precisely, with the uniform sheen of doll hair, and combed into place by someone who believed symmetry was credibility. His eyebrows were dyed a color that attempted to match the toupee, bushy but aggressively maintained, as if they were the last natural thing about him and therefore under strict supervision.

He looked like a man who, without daily intervention by a spouse or stylist, would collapse into chaos.

With it, he looked unstoppable.

No one would dare speak of the atrocity that sat on his scalp.

Robert spoke the way people do when they expect silence before they finish the sentence. He did not raise his voice. He simply assumed ownership of the room when he used it. He had flown in on one of his jets. He had several. Companies passed through his hands the way his beach houses did—acquired, improved, sold, replaced with something warmer and closer to water.

At his side was his assistant, Nancy.

Nancy was in her mid-fifties and functioned less like an executive assistant and more like an extension of William's nervous system. She had never married, had no children, no pets, and no visible life outside of managing William's. She lived on one of his properties. Which one changed depending on where Robert needed her.

Nancy was what you would imagine as an eighties rock band roadie would grow into. Hair still heavily hair-sprayed, large, and teased. Heavy, colorful blue eye liner and red lipstick. She used to be a chain smoker. Now she's equipped with a purse full of vapes, cycling through flavors that make her smell like a beach party threw up on her. Piña Colada, Cotton Candy, Cherry Explosion, Blue Razzmatazz. But her voice still carried the gravel of decades spent arguing with cigarettes.

Nothing was ever quite right for Nancy. Chairs were wrong. Temperatures were wrong. Agendas were wrong. People were wrong. Everything needed her adjustments and sign off. Nothing was off limits if it meant making Robert happy.

Tina usually had to take a Xanax anytime she knew she Nancy was coming. This had become standard practice since the private equity firm had acquired ASYS.

The rest of the board followed the chairman in a loose formation—black and gray suits, well enough fitted to signal success without implying excess. They spoke rarely and mostly nodded to prove they had a pulse. Most were in their sixties or seventies, poached from legacy banking boards. When they did speak, it was to agree with Robert, often before he finished the thought. They were mainly for show, versus any actual advice for the chairman.

Introductions were warm and vague.

Robert didn't sit down.

"So," he said, looking at no one in particular, "remind me what the core product does."

William answered first, as expected.

"It's a modern payments enablement platform," William said smoothly, hands open. "We abstract banking complexity and give enterprise clients a flexible way to move money globally, securely, and at scale."

Robert nodded once.

Eugene leaned in next, eager to add texture.

"At its heart," Eugene said, "ASYS is really about orchestration. We sit between legacy rails and emerging use cases, allowing clients to configure flows without needing to rebuild their stack."

Robert nodded again.

Declan waited a beat longer than necessary.

"It clears payments," he said. "Routes them. Settles them. Keeps regulators calm and customers unaware anything almost went wrong."

The room paused.

William smiled, thinly.

Eugene nodded, enthusiastically, as if that had been exactly what he meant.

Robert considered all three answers at once.

Payments enablement.

Orchestration layer.

Clearing and settlement with anxiety management.

Each answer was correct.

Together, they described three different companies that shared a logo.

Robert nodded anyway.

"Good," he said. "That's what I thought."

No one was entirely sure what that meant.

1:30 PM — The Avoidance Tour

For the next hour and a half, the board did not enter the boardroom.

Instead, they toured the headquarter campus.

They were escorted carefully through the back and sides of the building—the sides that faced the river. Windows overlooking the front lawn were avoided with subtle choreography. Hallways were selected based on sightlines. Doors were closed that were usually open.

No one explained why.

Outside, Robert walked the rear grounds and the brick-paved walk along the river approvingly, commenting on "the footprint" and "the setting," as if evaluating a future real estate listing. The river sparkled obligingly. Nancy hovered, tablet in hand, calling out local facts like a tour guide.

They ate lunch at the executive river club, The Swan, that sat conveniently next door.

It was a four-star restaurant. Members only.

Tony's would not be on the menu for this group.

Inside the building, HR and Security used the absence efficiently.

Landscaping personnel were moved quietly through side entrances, escorted past conference rooms and empty offices, carrying ropes, cones, and measuring tools. The front lawn was cordoned off with professional speed, the damage reframed as *an area under maintenance.*

Facilities sent no update.

No one asked.

By the time the board returned through the rear entrance, the lawn was quarantined, and Jackie's minions off to order a hefty list of materials.

At 2:59 PM, the boardroom doors finally closed.

The boardroom windows overlooked the river from the top floor. Nancy opened the freshly stocked boardroom fridge to distribute imported spring water to the visitors. Tina reached in afterwards to pull the regular bottled waters from the bottom shelf for the ASYS execs, then quietly departed stage left.

No one noticed the intern in the corner sitting quietly with their laptop, ready to assist if needed.

3:00 PM — The Board Meeting

The room was quiet. Quiet in a way that proved one person in the room had paychecks and careers in his hands.

Slides advanced before questions finished.

"Headcount feels high," one board member muttered.

Declan nodded immediately.

Jessica smiled tightly, slowly rubbing her eye so that the room would not notice the twitch.

"We're focused on operating efficiency," Eugene said.

The phrase **lean operating model** appeared on a slide.

No one defined it.

Another board member leaned forward.

"Tell me about resilience."

Thad was invited only because he had *Chief* in his title, and there could have been a technology-related question. He started to lean forward to respond, as the question sounded dangerously close to *cyber* resilience.

Eugene smiled and cut in. "Glad you asked."

The slide titled **Operational Resilience** appeared.

Thad leaned back in his chair along the back wall. He had come to the conclusion that the *C* in Chief Technology Officer was a little *c*. He then vowed to speak only if called by name for the remainder of this meeting.

A third board member adjusted his glasses.

"At the end of the day," he said, "what's our AI story?"

A slide titled **AI-Enabled Future State** appeared.

It contained three arrows, a cloud icon, and the word *Intelligent* twice.

William spoke about vision.

Eugene spoke about roadmaps.

Bob asked whether the compute costs were "material."

No one mentioned what the AI actually did.

Thad had nothing to do with the creation of this slide.

Nor would he be called on to expand on any details.

The board nodded.

"At the end of the day," another board member added, "it's about staying ahead."

No one disagreed.

Karen was invited to comment on regulation.

"The regulatory landscape remains dynamic," she said.

A slide listing regions and acronyms appeared. None were explained.

"At the end of the day," yet another board member said, "we want to be proactive."

Karen nodded. Proactive was safe.

Bob presented a chart showing cloud spend *flattening.*

Flattening compared to last quarter. Or last year. Or something.

"At the end of the day," Bob said, "we like the trend."

Declan nodded, even though the line was still going up.

A board member asked about customer segmentation.

"Who's the ideal customer now?"

Derrick said *mid-market enterprise.*

Declan said *upper SMB.*

William said *strategic partners.*

Three people wrote three different things in their notebooks.

"At the end of the day," Robert said mildly, "we're serving the right customers."

The board agreed.

A slide titled **Culture & Values** appeared.

Trust.

Accountability.

Velocity.

Someone asked how it was measured.

"Qualitatively," Jessica said.

The slide moved on quickly.

Talent retention came up next.

"Hiring feels tough," a board member observed.

"At the end of the day," another said, "people want meaning."

No one mentioned attrition.

The roadmap slide appeared.

It listed Q3, Q4, and **Beyond**.

Beyond took up half the slide.

"At the end of the day," Eugene said, "we feel confident."

Thad shifted in his chair and did not speak. He couldn't wipe the smile from his face thinking about what all was happening "at the end of the day" with this group.

Incident preparedness was discussed.

"How ready are we?" someone asked.

"Very," William said.

"At the end of the day," Declan added, "we've got muscle memory."

Thad crossed his arms. His thunder stolen. His purpose in the meeting quickly dropping to zero.

A competitor was mentioned vaguely.

"I read something last week," a board member said.

No one knew what.

Marketing assured everyone they were differentiated.

The slide said **Competitive Advantage**.

There were no logos.

Metrics flashed by—uptime, throughput, transaction volume.

All green.

All unlabeled.

"At the end of the day," someone said, "green is good."

No one challenged that.

Thad now stared blankly. His remaining purpose of being there now completely gone. He did not create the system metrics slides, and was not sure where the data came from, or if even accurate.

Near the end, Robert asked, "Anything you need from us?"

"Continued support," William said.

Everyone nodded, relieved.

4:18 PM — The Question That Almost Lands

A board member asked, casually, "Were there any customer impacts recently?"

The room paused.

Thad tightened his lips, crossed his arms, and committed to his goal of not speaking unless called on.

William answered smoothly.

"We experienced a brief stress test," he said. "Minimal impact. Strong response."

The board nodded.

Nancy wrote *Handled well* in her notebook.

"At the end of the day," she whispered to no one.

Thad's face turned a shade of light rage, but remained steady.

5:40 PM — Fallout

The board left satisfied.

Action items were assigned vaguely.

Thad updated the teams channel one last time.

— — —

[Teams | Payments War Room – Lite]

Reynolds, Thad (5:40 PM)
Board meeting concluded.
No changes requested.
I said 0 words.
Tech slides existed. I didn't create them.
Continue monitoring.

— Ortega, Sam reacted with shock —
— Brooks, Evan reacted with a facepalm —

— — —

Maya closed her laptop carefully.

The intern watched the dashboards.
They stayed green.

Thursday ended with exhaustion.

Friday would be about culture.

And culture, everyone knew, could fix anything.

FRIDAY: "Culture Day"

We're a family here!

8:30 AM — Company-Wide Email

The email from the marketing department arrived early enough to feel intentional. It was from Lily, the content manager, but was obviously from Jessica and edited to be "pretty" from the marketing team as one part of a bigger social media campaign. The email was formatted like a thank you card, and had a pastel blue background, with images of doves and "Thank You" in light colors that did well not to overpower the text.

— — —

[Email]

From: Harper, Lily
Subject: Moving Forward Together

Team,

I want to take a moment to acknowledge the resilience, adaptability, and professionalism demonstrated this week.

Moments like these remind us who we are when things get complex. Our values guide us, our people rise, and our culture carries us forward.

Thank you for showing up for one another.

Please remember to take time today to recharge and reconnect.

With gratitude,

Jessica Lane
Chief People Officer

— — —

The email was well received.

Several people reacted with hearts in Outlook.

One person forwarded it to their personal email address, blatantly disregarding the security protocol.

Someone else read it twice, looking for instructions for how to recharge. Some text that translated to go home early, or that there was cake in the front lobby as a thank you.

None were present.

9:15 AM — The Lawn

Facilities sent another message.

— — —

[Email]

From: Facilities

Subject: Grounds Update

The front lawn will remain temporarily closed as we complete scheduled maintenance.

Please use alternate walkways when entering or exiting the building.

— — —

No one replied or acknowledged.

By now, the tire tracks had been partially covered, but replaced with obvious track shaped lined of new sod bordered in white sand used for levelling the turf. The front marquee was cleaned, with no signs of mud slung from the chaos. Cones marked the perimeter. Yellow tape fluttered optimistically. A row of new bushes and flowers from the local nursery sat along the front drive, ready to be planted.

Marketing would later refer to this as *a campus entrance refresh.*

10:00 AM — Recognition Segment

An impromptu all-hands meeting for on-site employees was called.

Everyone at the campus was asked to join the executive team in the auditorium for a *special message.* The phrasing alone caused a measurable drop in productivity. Some people avoided going entirely, convinced it was a cover for coming layoffs. Others stayed at their desks because they hadn't read the email, or had read it and decided ignorance was still preferable.

The auditorium filled unevenly. Most everyone sat along the back of the room, except the row of senior leaders and direct reports to the C-Suite. The technology team sat together by the AV booth in the back so that they could chat amongst themselves.

Other groups sat together like cliques in high school. *Melrose Place* sat close to the exit, non-subtly surrounded by men from various departments.

The meeting turned out to be a recognition segment.

This came as a surprise to nearly everyone, including several of the senior leaders in the front row.

A single slide appeared on the large background screen:

This Week's Wins – Thank You!

The font was cheerful. Almost aggressive.

Derrick spoke first.

"I just want to call out the incredible teamwork we've seen," he said. "So many people stepping up."

He gestured to the screen.

A list of Marketing and Sales names followed.

Two no longer worked there.

One had resigned quietly on Tuesday.

Another had been escorted out Wednesday afternoon. Something about coming into the office extremely hung over from a client outing the night before, puking at his desk, and passing out, only to be found by one of Jackie's minions after lunch.

Their achievements remained intact.

Derrick continued.

"These folks really embody momentum," he said. A few folks laughed out loud, followed by a cough for cover.

Jessica clapped politely. Eugene nodded without looking up from his phone.

Next came Bob.

Bob approached the podium with a printed sheet of paper he had clearly prepared himself. He thanked Finance for "navigating complexity," which was his preferred phrase for *nothing went catastrophically wrong.* He named people in alphabetical order, pausing briefly after each name, as if expecting applause to emerge organically.

It did not.

One name was pronounced wrong.

Another belonged to someone currently on extended leave for recent events in the front lawn. Whispers were louder than the uncomfortable movement in seats.

A third person that was called out was in the room, and raised a hand from the back and mouthed *I'm not in Finance.*

Bob thanked them anyway.

"At the end of the day," he said, "it's about discipline."

Karen followed.

She did not thank individuals. She thanked functions. She was stern, and methodical. Zero emotion in the delivery.

Legal. Risk. External Counsel.

She thanked them for "holding the line" and "protecting the enterprise." No one was sure what they had been protected from, but the implication felt expensive.

Jessica was next.

She stood, smiled, and delivered gratitude with surgical precision. She thanked people for *care*, *empathy*, and *handling difficult conversations.* Several attendees flinched. Two looked down at their shoes. Emily left to take a fake call.

Her list was accurate and thoughtful.

Then Eugene stood.

He thanked everyone.

All of them.

"Across the board," he said, "this was a team effort."

He did not name anyone.

This went on.

Declan walked up for Operations.

He thanked his customer support team for "being agile," which meant *they responded to his emails quickly.*

Slides advanced. Applause happened in pockets. The hour stretched.

Finally, Thad's name appeared on the agenda.

This surprised him.

Tina had called him late the night before and asked to "add a few names," which he had done carefully, cross-checking employment status and recent events. He did not realize he would actually get to say anything himself. He approached the stage quickly, navigating to the podium, adjusting the microphone he didn't need. He had went with his white Zelda hoodie, jeans, and black Chucks that day. It was a fit choice chosen for not presenting on stage.

"I'll keep this short," he said.

The room quieted. Everyone liked Thad, and gave him the attention the other execs wished for. Thad was unaware, but the other execs noticed and were jealous.

"I want to thank my Infrastructure, Applications, and Security teams," he said. "Specifically the people who were **awake.**"

Evans head popped up.

"You know who you are," he added. "You don't need a slide."

He named names. All current. All correct.

The intern scanned the list. His name did not appear. He wasn't surprised. He still checked twice.

Noticing them in the crowd, Thad felt bad and added, "Although not listed, I will say that our intern did a great job this week too." He said it briefly, without embellishment. The intern blushed and smiled.

"And for everyone else," Thad continued, "if you didn't see your name today, that doesn't mean your work wasn't critical. You're all crucial."

A few people nodded. One laughed softly.

He paused.

"This week was… interesting," he said. "While some of us were in meetings, others were fixing things. Quietly. In the background. That mattered. And I really appreciate you."

He did not mention issues or recovery.

He didn't need to.

"Anyway," Thad said, stepping back, "thank you, again. The systems are stable. **No more latency**." He winked at his team as he hurried back off stage.

Applause followed. Real this time.

The meeting ended with a final note from Tina on a Happy hour event coming up at lunch.

People filed out slowly, unsure what they had just witnessed, but faintly reassured. No one got laid off today.

12:00 PM — Forced Fun

The calendar invite had said *Optional.*

Attendance suggested otherwise.

— — —

[Calendar Invite]

Virtual Happy Hour
Duration: 45 minutes
Agenda: Connect

— — —

The meeting was a mix of onsite and virtual. The food was setup in the large conference room. The room was much smaller than the auditorium, but with it being *Virtual* and *Optional*, the expectation was that most would join via video from their desks, or remote for those not in the office. This was a poor assumption. The crowd poured out into the hallway as the team waited for their chance for free food. Cake, popcorn, pizza, and even a new offering from Tony's menu: cheeseburgers. A few fell for the bait and grabbed the tinfoil-wrapped sandwiches. But once they were opened, and the stale bun, thin mystery meat patty, and almost transparent slice of cheese was revealed, the rest of the line made sure to bypass that section of the table.

People that joined virtually joined with cameras off, so that they could enjoy their alcoholic drinks in peace. Someone accidentally turned on a filter and spent the entire call as a potato without acknowledging it. Another had joined via their cell phone on mute and had their camera on without knowing it, and onlookers watched as they walked around their home, doing their laundry, passing by a mirror showing that they were in their underwear, and finally stopping by the restroom.

"BILLY, TURN OFF YOUR CAMERA!" Jessica yelled, praying that he heard her before he committed to the restroom break and violated a few exposure laws. Billy dropped completely.

She collected herself, and continued

"So anyway… Just wanted to create a little space today," she said. "It's been a week."

Bob joined late via video, already holding a drink. He didn't care he was on camera. He had left the all-hands and went directly home to hop on the call and eat at home.

Derrick had a branded background. He sipped on an Arnold Palmer and prepping for his next round with another client for that afternoon.

Eugene appeared in the conference room for three minutes.

"Love this energy," he said. "Really proud of the culture here." He immediately left.

No one spoke. Everyone enjoyed the pizza, cake, and popcorn. Facilities would be cleaning up uneaten burgers later.

IT and Security did not attend. Thad had already brought in real food for the group and they ate together in the network operations center. Thad stopped by the conference room to represent the group for a few minutes, chatted with a few people from various other departments, and came back to his team.

Jessica and Lily stopped by the operations center to chat with Thad and sit with the IT and security teams for a few minutes to show their appreciation.

The virtual attendees had disconnected around 12:30 PM. The onsite crowd dispersed exactly at 1:00 PM. Many would disappear for the remainder of the day, assuming it would go unnoticed.

2:30 PM — Quiet Consequences

The intern was performing some routine access log checks based on the runbook. More access changes showed up for a few.

No announcements were made. No emails were sent. No meeting was scheduled to explain it. No tickets were opened for tracking. Nothing could be argued with.

A few permissions simply disappeared.

Alex and Jordan lost access to all production systems they used for the job functions. This was expected, but there would normally at least be a ticket from HR for closing out access. The situation was unique based on who was involved, but it felt weird that there would be a complete bypass of the process.

The intern's permissions had changed too.

A shared folder had become read-only.

Jira tickets assigned to the intern were reassigned to Sam and Noah by Evan. Ownership moved sideways, then down, then settled somewhere neutral.

The intern refreshed a page in Visual Studio he had open.

The *Deploy* functions were gone.

They refreshed again, slower this time, as if speed had caused the problem. The page came back exactly the same. They checked another system. Read-only. Another. Read-only again.

They waited.

Nothing changed, except their scope of responsibility.

The intern could no longer push changes to production. The permission had not been revoked dramatically; it had simply been removed, as if it had never been intended in the first place.

At the same time, other doors opened.

Logs he'd never been able to see before were suddenly available. Dashboards expanded. Systems that used to respond with *access denied* now loaded without complaint. They could observe more than ever. They just couldn't change anything.

It was expanded responsibility disguised as a restriction. Or a restriction disguised as trust.

They stared at the screen for a moment longer than necessary, then closed the tab.

They did not ask anyone about it.

They did not open a ticket.

They did not assume it was an accident.

They assumed that Thad was putting in guardrails, but still allowing them to learn and to grow. Like a parent putting up bumper guards around the house for the newborn.

They understood. No one yelled. No one explained. Permissions shifted. Roles adjusted themselves. Consequences were enforced quietly. But they felt that there was still a silver lining in that they were given more freedom to look around, and help look for other problems they could help fix. Somehow.

3:00 PM — Finance "Team" Panic

With the latency issue resolved, standard transaction traffic returned.

Which meant the numbers changed again.

Rachel noticed immediately. She always did. The variance wasn't subtle this time. It was the kind of swing that made all of the decks from this week obsolete and assumptions made during conversations with the board embarrassing. A correction large enough to matter, but small enough that no one would remember *why* it happened by Monday.

Emails were sent.

Not panicked ones. Not accusatory ones. Calm, clipped questions that implied answers already existed and Rachel was simply behind on acknowledging them.

Can you re-run this?

Just want to sanity check the model.

These numbers feel off.

She rebuilt the model for the fourth time that week.

She adjusted inputs. Rebalanced assumptions. Updated footnotes no one read. She fixed formulas that had never been wrong but now needed to look different because reality had changed again.

At 3:07 PM, she sent Bob an update.

At 3:12 PM, Bob replied with a single line.

"thanks let's use the updated version have a good weekend"

No punctuation. No acknowledgment of the hours. No question about why it had changed. The model existed only to be correct, not to be appreciated.

Rachel stared at the message for a moment longer than necessary, then closed it.

She glanced at Teams.

It was 3:00 PM on a Friday.

Her team channel was silent. No typing indicators. No reactions. No one pretending to still be online. They had all already gone home. It was comically on trend for the accounting and finance team to disappear by 3:00 PM every Friday, knowing nothing urgent will be officially urgent until Monday. Coincidentally, 3:00 PM was also when Eugene, Bob, and William were "In meetings the rest of the day."

Rachel stayed.

She always did.

She finalized the model. Renamed the file. Added *FINAL_v4* to the end, knowing full well it would not be final and that *v5* would arrive uninvited sometime before breakfast on Monday by someone.

At 3:48 PM, she closed Excel.

At 3:49 PM, she opened a different document.

Her resignation letter.

It had been started weeks ago, also on a Friday around 4:00 PM, then paused, then revised in small, careful increments. Today she adjusted a sentence, softened a phrase, removed a line that sounded too emotional and replaced it with one that sounded objective and professional enough to be ignored.

She saved it.

At 4:30 PM, she shut down her laptop.

She printed the letter. Folded it once, cleanly. Placed it on Bob's empty desk, centered, aligned with the edge like it was part of the furniture. His name clearly printed on the outside.

No drama.

Just another number that had changed.

Rachel turned off her light and left.

Finance would notice Monday.

Eventually.

4:45 PM — "Have a Great Weekend!"

The day technically ended at five.

Which made the timing notable.

Eugene sent the email himself, from home, having decided earlier that afternoon to work remote "to stay focused." The message arrived just early enough to imply generosity, but late enough to be useless.

For hourly employees, it implied they had been granted fifteen minutes of freedom.

For the rest of the company, it arrived after they had already left or stopped checking emails.

The email was brief. Cheerful. Earnest.

— — —

[Email]
From: Caldwell, Eugene
Subject: Have a Great Weekend!

Team,

Thank you again for the focus and dedication this week.

Please take time to unplug and recharge.

See you Monday,
Eugene

Sent from iPhone

— — —

The phrase *unplug and recharge* lingered on screens still connected to incident channels, dashboards, and half-written follow-ups.

No one replied.

No one forwarded it.

A few people read it twice, checking the timestamp to confirm it hadn't been delayed.

It had not.

Teams messages continued.

Alerts were acknowledged.

Someone asked if a change could wait until Monday and received no answer, which they correctly interpreted as *no.*

At 4:59 PM, Sam committed hotfix code.

At 5:03 PM, Evan smoke tested the push.

The weekend had technically begun.

Operationally, it had not.

Eugene's email remained unread by most, quietly implying gratitude, rest, and closure—three things no one in the building associated with that week.

5:15 PM — Still Online

People logged off performatively.

Status dots flipped from green to yellow in deliberate waves, as if visibility itself needed to be managed. A few goodbyes were sent. Several people simply stopped responding mid-conversation, the digital equivalent of an Irish goodbye.

Some green dots remained.

They always did.

In IT, the ones still online weren't lingering by accident. They were wrapping up just enough to justify stopping. Closing tabs. Clearing sessions. Leaving systems stable in a way that suggested intention, not neglect.

In **IT General**, one final question appeared.

— — —

[Teams | IT General]

Natarajan, Priya (5:16 PM)
Can we remove the workaround from Monday?

Ortega, Sam (5:17 PM)
Let's not rush it, please.

— — —.

No one reacted.

Everyone understood.

The intern closed their laptop carefully, the way you do when you've learned that machines remember how you treat them. They didn't rush. They didn't double-check. If something was wrong now, it would still be wrong later, and if it wasn't, they weren't going to break it on a Friday.

One by one, the remaining IT team members signed off.

Seven o'clock gambling was coming.

Poker night required a different kind of readiness. A mental switch. No more wasted gray matter for incident bridges, dashboards, and postmortems. People were preparing themselves for cards, cash, loud music, booze, inappropriate jokes, and the agreed-upon fiction that work did not exist for several hours.

Friday ended the way it always did.

Exhausted.

Between the parking lot and their cars, the weight of the week lifted off of their shoulders. The weekend was here.

Outside, the cones remained around the destroyed front lawn, glowing orange in the early evening light. No one touched them. That was a Monday problem.

FRIDAY NIGHT: "Poker Night"

This is the climax!

7:05 PM – First Arrivals

Thad answered the door in mid-calf socks, carpenter shorts, and a freshly washed Call of Duty T-shirt.

People arrived in uneven waves—late, very late, some half-drunk already. Some knocked politely. Others just walked in shouting "We're here!" Everyone knew the code. Thad hugged some people, nodded at or shook hands with others, and immediately handed the intern a drink he hadn't asked for.

"Survived your first week?" Thad asked casually.

The intern blinked. "Barely."

"Yeah," Thad said. "That tracks."

They drifted toward the kitchen so that the intern could sit down the chips and dip they had brought, thinking it was customary. As if remembering something important, Thad added, quieter, "Hey—sorry about the permission changes. I figured you'd already figured it out."

The intern nodded. He had. "Yeah, I understand the *'Why*"

"Good," Thad said. "You'll do well here, if you decide to stick around once the internship program ends." He added, " But for now, you ready to lose some money at the card table?"

"Sure, I played a bit with friend in college," the intern responded.

"This isn't a kid's game. You better be prepared to get your feelings hurt and your money taken," Thad said sternly, but then quickly turned to a smile proving the sarcastic, but somewhat serious message.

Trying to continue the conversation with his chief officer, the intern continued, "So, this week was crazy. Married folks fooling around at work, getting caught, folks destroying the landscaping, and the police showing up? That was nuts."

Thad laughed.

"Oh," he said, waving a hand. "I guess no one told you what ASYS really stands for, huh?"

The intern froze. "No?"

Thad leaned in conspiratorially. "**Always Sharing Your Spouse.**"

The intern choked on his drink.

"I'm serious," Thad continued while smiling. "We've had… multiple occurrences."

He began counting on his fingers.

"Earlier this year, there was the legal admin who was sleeping with the marketing director in the parking garage. She got fired. He didn't. Have you met Tom Willis yet?"

"What? Yes, I met him. The communications guy, right? Why didn't he get fired too?"

"He's related to William. Cousin or something."

A beat.

"And then," Thad added, "there's our own famous *seven couples.*"

7:35 PM — The Seven Couples

"Back when I started having poker nights every Friday," Thad said, refilling drinks, "seven married couples used to come over consistently, among others. These couples were all employees of the company. You know, small town with only a few large companies to work for here."

He paused. Someone had turned up the music, so Thad would have to speak louder. The music was a mix of 90's and 2000's Rap, pop, metal, and the occasional country song that would slip in. The mix only made sense to Thad. When the bass hit right, Thad couldn't help make his "stank face," and bob his head. As more drinks were consumed throughout the night, the face and head bobs would evolve into his "killer" dance moves. At least he thought they were great.

"Anyway, fast-forward a few years… Those seven couples turned into four new couples. Same people. Different combinations. Three divorces. No overlap paperwork... We think."

The intern stared wide-eyed.

"Evan and his wife made it," Thad said. "Lily and I still going strong."

"Everyone else," he shrugged, "optimized. Most should be here tonight."

"Wait… Lily? Harper? The content manager that sent out the email this week?" The intern asked, trying not to choke on their drink.

"Oh. Um, yeah," Thad paused. "We met at work during a manager training and got married like 6 months later. She wanted me, bad!"

He let the joke sit to allow it to be appreciated.

The intern smiled politely.

Thad continued, "No, seriously, I had to convince her. Beg a little, even. I married up. She kept her maiden name at work so that folks wouldn't easily make the connection. I guess it still works. We try to keep em separated while at work. That was a 90's music reference, by the way" He said with a wink.

The intern smiled politely again, not getting the reference.

8:00 PM — (Frat) House Rules

Both the dealer and the bartender of the party were young fraternity brothers from Thad's alma mater at the local university. Thad would call the Sigma Nu house for these events in case any of the younger guys, or even the pledges needed some extra cash.

They knew the rules.

What happens here, stays here.

One kept the drinks filled and the cooler stocked.

The other dealt cards and yelled out drink orders for the table. It was a system that worked well, and was cheap compared to using an official bartending service. Thad would normally tip well, as send them off with a case of their favorite beer as well.

8:04 PM — Evan and Valeria

Evan entered abruptly without knocking, flanked by his wife, Valeria, a Panamanian woman, fierce, tattooed like a walking mural. "We're here!" Evan yelled out.

Valeria kissed Thad on the cheek, slapped Evan on his butt in a flirty way for something he hadn't done yet, and immediately asked Thad where the chips and dip were.

Valeria was younger, sharper, louder. She swore fluently in two languages and played poker like she was settling personal scores. Evan was shorter, around 5' 6", but muscular, shaved bald head, beard perfectly manicured, and hovered near his wife like a loyal satellite. She stood at 5' 2", but the 3" heels levelled the playing field.

They had met in in Costa Rica while both were travelling with their respective friends. He had followed her around the entire trip. She followed him home. They had been joined at the hip ever since.

"She's my world," Evan told the intern proudly as he walked by, "even when that world is on fire, and yelling at me. I'm right where I want to be."

They handed their drinks of choice to Thad to put in the fridge and went directly to the poker table as the dealer was tossing out the first hand of the night. Valeria pushed Evan's cards to him, straightened them for him, without looking at the cards or him. She folded up the corners of her cards to see what was delivered. No reaction. The others already sitting at the table knew to fear her, and that they would not get a read.

8:22 PM — Thad's Family (Off-Site)

As if she heard her name mentioned, Thad's wife, Lily Harper, walked from the back bedroom to welcome the guests that had made it. She had just finished up getting dressed and ready to be seen by friends.

"Hello!" she said in a sweet voice to the intern. "Welcome to the Reynold's house! I hear this was your first big week at ASYS that involved board members coming, and the big drama outside all in one week."

"Yes, it was *interesting*," the intern responded.

"That's certain one word for it. Unfortunately, it may not be the last time you get to witness that kind of fun there."

She made eye contact with Thad, then the cooler. He promptly went to refilled the ice.

She nodded toward the trash. He took it out.

She lifted one eyebrow. A half-finished crass joke with Evan went silent. It took about 20 years, but Thad was now fairly trained.

Their kids were gone for the night. Lily was making the intern feel welcome and getting them familiar with the family.

"Our oldest, Kat, is pre-med at the local college," she told the intern softly. "Our younger son, JT, is still in high school and practices day-trading on the Japanese markets at night after baseball practice. He's planning to be a millionaire before he's twenty."

Thad added, proudly, "Between the two of them, our retirement should be set."

"WOOOO, ALL IN, BABY!" Evan yells in the background.

"I CALL, BEEYATCH!" his wife fires back at him quickly.

"Oh Lord, they've already started," sighed Lily.

"That's on par for them. They've already been here almost 30 minutes. I'm surprised they waited that long to open up," Thad added, winking at the intern.

8:25 PM — The Sound of Silence

Sam arrived with his fiancée, Raven Chen. Chen, as in Maya's younger sister. The couple did not match at all. Sam was a medium build guy of Spanish decent. His family had been in the states for a few generations, so the only Spanish he knew was "gracias" and "Adiós." He dressed casually, like most of the engineers. Regular fit jeans, colorful sneakers, and a loose fitting thin hoodie with the name of some Indie band unknown to the group. He had a scruffy face, as he only shaved once a week, and his straight black hair fell loosely into his eyes, constantly having to blow it back.

Raven, as the name suggested, was dark. All black, except the porcelain makeup that accented her Asian complexion. Her platform knee-high boots gave her a good thee inches of height. The net stockings accompanied what looked like a repurposed maid's uniform. Black stone and pewter jewelry layers on her neck and fingers, as if she got a bulk discount at Hot Topic. Her hair pulled up into two ponytails, with fang shaped bangs bordering each side of her slim face. Her eye shadow was a dark gradient from black to navy blue. Her lipstick the same menacing gradient but from a black outer border to a blood red center.

Raven rarely left Sam's side. He greeted Thad at the door, handed him a six pack of a local draft brew, and walked straight top the poker table. Evan and Valeria greeted them with a smile and silence, as they were already betting hard on the current hand. The crowd tried not to stare. Sam had been dating Raven for a few months, and they had seen her in even wilder cosplay outfits at other functions, but it was still always a shock to see the two together. Sam definitely had a type. He loved the anime streamer girls. They gamed together. She sat closely beside him. She didn't drink. She didn't speak.

Sam would ask occasionally if she needed anything.

She would shake her head or whisper something in his ear. On occasion you would see Sam giggle like a little kid at something she said to him, but she made no facial expression to signify that it was something meant to be funny.

Sam sipped on his craft beer, and focused on playing poker.

8:47 PM — Jessica Exists In Real Life

Jessica arrived. HR Jessica.

The intern nearly spilled his drink.

Thad laughed. "Relax. We're friends."

Jessica was… different. Instead of the tight bun, her long blonde hair was in a ponytail. Long sleeve sheer white blouse, spaghetti strap tank top showing through the top, black leggings, white Adidas that looked as though they were bedazzled on the back. Laughing loudly as if she had been holding it in all week.

In one hand was a large white Yeti, filled with her vino of choice. On her other shoulder rested her oversized purse with the top of two red wine bottles peering out. She was prepared for a long night. She swore a bit. Not like a sailor, but enough to make it feel weird to hear coming from the head of HR. As the night went on, she would dance badly, tell funny stories, and show that she was a completely different person than the calm and quiet executive at work.

"This is who she is," Thad said, pointing at Jessica as she talked to Lily. "Work Jessica is a costume. She is one of the divorcees of the seven couples that did not remarry. Her ex is no longer with the company. It is safe to say she had a hand in that. Don't tell her I said that. He was a douche. He was only ever allowed to come to my house because he was married to her."

The intern recalibrated reality. They couldn't tell if that statement was comforting or more of a warning.

9:12 PM — Derrick, Already Gone

Derrick arrived half-drunk from golf with clients and planned to continue the festivities with his real friends.

"God, I needed this," he said, hugging Thad and Jessica like college friends. "Wadup, fam?"

The intern's internal org chart collapsed completely.

"Dude, you're already hammered? You couldn't drink slower on the course since you knew you were coming here?" Thad asked with a smile.

"Get off my ass, Thaddeus. I'm fine."

"Don't call me that. Only my mother calls me that… or Lily if she's **really** mad at me," Thad responded with a playful punch to Derricks shoulder.

"Boys, play nice," Lily said calmly and motherly.

"Hey," Derrick continued, "You really gotta speak up in those exec calls man. Don't let them walk all over you."

"What's the point? Those two are the fifth and sixth CEO's we have had since I started working for that place. They won't last another year, and we will have someone else to suck up to that has no idea what I am talking about when I talk about anything important. Sir Robert BuysALot will find a replacement for them as soon as he finds someone else that will potentially make the stock price go up a dollar," Thad said in one breath.

Derrick nodded in agreement, and gave an apologetic smile and pat on the shoulder for accidentally bringing up work. He handed Thad a handle of Crown that he brought with him that was a third empty from the course. Thad would find a spot in the back of the fridge that it wouldn't be messed with by others.

Evan was already down to his last few chips. His head slumped in shame. He looked over at his wife's stack of chips. She met his glance, smiled and threw a kiss at him, to make him feel a little better, but not so much as to make him think she would start going easy on him. The game wasn't over yet. The tide could turn.

9:38 PM — Priya and the Accessory

Priya showed up late, trailing a guy who was technically her boyfriend, though "arm candy" was probably more accurate.

He was in his late twenties, Italian, and looked like he spent more on his hair gel than most people do on rent. His white shirt was buttoned so low it was basically just a cape for his chiseled, tanned chest, which was, of course, perfectly manicured. He had on black slacks and Italian red-bottomed shoes that looked like they'd never touched actual pavement. No socks, obviously. His slicked-back hair was blindingly shiny, and he was wearing a gold watch the size of a dinner plate that looked ready to give someone a tan if the light hit it wrong.

Priya looked like a completely different person. At work, she was the "safe" InfoSec boss who wore baggy sweaters and loose linen pants, looking like she wanted to blend into the office furniture. Tonight? She was a full-blown Bollywood goddess.

She was squeezed into a red dress that was tight in all the right places, trimmed in heavy gold beading that made her warm Indian skin look amazing. Her hair was dead-straight, black, and glossy enough to see your reflection in. With her big gold earrings and matching necklace, she looked less like she was heading to a poker game and more like she was about to accept a Lifetime Achievement Award.

The two of them stood in the middle of the living room looking aggressively expensive and totally out of place.

"Look at you, hottie! Is this the guy? The post-divorce guy from the bar?" Jessica yelled, way too loud, immediately blowing Priya's cool.

Jessica's wine had obviously already started to work its magic. The date smiled a confidence smile, not an embarrassed one.

Priya blushed a little, smiled, and rubbed her hand down his muscular chest. "He makes my ex furious."

The intern learned later she'd just bought her young boyfriend's outfit with alimony money that afternoon before the party. This was another of the 'seven' that had gotten a divorce but not yet remarried. She had not intended to date a younger man, but had obviously been caught up in the excitement and energy of his youth and interest in her. She had unintentionally become a "sugar mama."

10:15 PM — Noah Is Already Done

Noah arrived drunk.

He and his roommate had pre-gamed. Hard.

By 9:30 PM, he was done playing poker. By 10:15 PM, he was hunch over his roommate that he had invited to come along, telling a story about his ex-girlfriend, a sorority girl from the school he had recently graduated from the year before. She was still in her senior year and now with an offensive lineman on the football team, who was attending on a full scholarship. Noah was pitiful, and slightly sobbing as he put back another IPA. The roommate looked as though he was stoned out of his mind, and just kept repeating, "that sucks, bro."

12:18 AM — Pool Logic

Sam lost a bet to Evan, and half his stack with it.

Evan and Valeria were trading chips back and forth on each hand, battling for who would come out on top. The young Italian date sat with a stern face, frustrated at his performance, and even more that the loud Panamanian was kicking his ass at poker. Evan was proud and aggravated at the same time.

Thad was on his last five bucks. He called All-In blindly to end the suffering.

Valeria called him, since it would put him out.

Everyone else folded to watch Evan's wife take down their boss.

The flop was laid. Then the turn. Finally the river. No pairs on the table, or enough of the same suit to make any difference. A, 2, 7, 9, & 3 of mixed suits laid out in front of them.

"Flip'em," Valeria said quickly.

Thad turned over a 2 of hearts, and 5 of clubs.

"HA!" Valeria exclaimed as she turned over a 3 of diamonds and a Jack of Spades.

"I lost with a freaking pair of threes?" Thad asked as he slapped his forehead in disbelief. He added jokingly, "And in my own home?! How dare you?!"

Thad now felt that the pool should became relevant.

Shirts and shoes became optional. Laughter got louder. Alcohol-powered confidence elevated.

Thad started off the water activities by climbed the diving board. As he ran toward the end of the board and started a front flip, he partially pulled down his shorts to moon the crowd mid-flip before over rotating and hitting the water with a full belly flop.

Applause, cheers, and laughter from the guys, accompanied by looks of by the women similar to teenage girls looking at boys with a look of immature disgust. One specific look made Thad realize he needed to tone it down. He straighten up, tied his shorts tight, got out of the pool, and helped Lily empty the trash can. She didn't say a word.

Only one or two other guys decided to jump into the pool. The Italian jumped in, boxers only, since he had just been pushed out of the game by Evan's card shark of a wife. This caused a group of ladies to stand close by the pool and chat amongst themselves, while enjoying the view.

"Back up ladies. He's mine!" Priya exclaimed jokingly.

"We're just window shopping, girl," Jessica quickly replied. She leaned over Priya's shoulder, working to keep her balance, as she sipped hard from a giant straw from her Yeti that almost missed her mouth.

12:58 AM – Lucky Hand

It was getting close to 1:00 AM in the morning, and the three left standing in the card game was Sam, Evan, and Valeria. Sam's fiancée still sat quietly and patiently next to Sam, occasionally checking social media for any likes on her recent cosplay videos. She would stand up occasionally to refill their sodas and stretch her legs. Each time she came back to the table, she would rub Sam's back and shoulders to let him know she was there, and occasionally whisper in his ear. His face would light up more each time she said something, like a build up to something exciting.

The remaining three players' stacks were almost even. Each hand simply moving an equal amount of chips between players. The dealer was exhausted. He needed to study for a final that was coming up Monday, so he was looking forward to the game ending, getting paid, and going to bed.

Then came the hand.

Each player received their two cards.

Evan looked first. A pair of Kings.

Then Sam. 7-2 off-suite.

Finally, Valeria. Pocket Aces.

Her poker face held. She had this in the bag.

Sam's fiancé leaned over and whispered something in his ear. His eyes got very wide this time, and he blushed. "Um, ALL-IN!"

"Seriously?" Evan asked. "You sure about that?"

"Oh yeah. Very sure. I need to be somewhere," he said nonchalantly as he glanced over at his fiancé who was now looking down at her phone in her lap, slightly blushing.

"Ooooh, I get it. Nice!" Valeria stated, turning Sam's fiancée's face a full shade of red through the white makeup. She continued, "Ev, take note. You may get a similar whisper in the ear if I win!"

"Val, c'mon, man! Don't play with me like that. I want to win too!" Evan said, confused as to what he should do with a pair of Kings now. This is what you would call as being "put on tilt,"

"I call," Evan decided reluctantly.

"OK, I guess I am calling too," Valeria added.

The room was now quiet. Everyone was watching the action.

They flipped their cards to show what Sam had sacrificed to go home with his fiancée as requested.

"A seven-two off-suit? You definitely just gave up to go home." Valeria poked.

"Yup," Sam replied.

Raven blushed again, with a slight smile creeping up on the corners of her black and red lips.

Evan flipped his pocket kings. He quickly looked at his wife, thinking he had a chance. He wanted to get some sort of reaction.

She made no facial response. She looked Evan dead in the eyes, and didn't break contact as she flipped over her pocket Aces. Evan broke eye contact to look down.

"NOOOOO!!" Evan cried, along with cheers and yelling from the crowd.

First the flop.

7, 5, 4. Total garbage flop. Everyone agreed that it was awful.

Then came the Turn. A king!

"Wooo Hooo!" Evan exclaimed. But he was conflicted. He was about to beat his wife at poker. That had not happened in weeks. But it also meant that he probably used his last bit of luck on that poker hand, vs getting lucky at home.

"Keep cheering, buddy boy. You haven't won yet. And if you do, you still lose!" Valeria said as he winked at her husband. She already knew that regardless of the outcome he would have a good night. She just liked playing with her prey beforehand.

No one moved or changed facial expression. The dealer couldn't flip the River card fast enough.

Ace of Spades.

The room erupted as if they were watching the World Series of Poker, or a last minute touchdown to win a Superbowl.

"DAAAMMIITT!!" Evan screamed, slumping onto the table, burying his head into his arms.

Valeria stood up, and walked around the table victorious, relishing every ounce of her husband's defeat. She lifted her hands in the air as if asking the group if they were not entertained. As she came back around the table, she leaned over against Evan's back, put her arms around him, and whispered into his ear, "Now let's go home so you can win."

"Yes, ma'am. Bye Thaddeus! We're out!" Evan said hastily, as he grabbed his wife's hand, an almost empty bottle of Jack, and rushed out the door.

"Um, well, bye!" Thad yelled as they shut the door, doubtful they heard him say anything.

4:02 AM — Closing Time Survivors

By four in the morning, the house had entered its final state.

Quiet. Settled. The way places do when nothing else is going to happen, and everyone who could leave already had.

Derrick was passed out by the pool, sprawled out on a pool chair, feet hanging over onto the concrete, holding an empty bottle of Crown like a teddy bear. His sunglasses were still on.

Jessica had taken a guest room to pass out. Her empty wine bottles rested by the door. She would help Lily clean up the next morning. After taking a handful of ibuprofen that Lily had placed on the night stand in preparation.

The couples were long gone.

They had peeled off either very publicly after the poker game, or naturally, in pairs, sometime between midnight and two, disappearing into ride-shares and shared glances. There may have been some formation of future secretive work couples that had happened throughout the night. Whatever they'd come to forget had been forgotten.

Priya and her accessory had left around 1:30 AM.

The Italian had convinced her that the club downtown was still open until six. She sighed deeply, said she was too old for this, but then went anyway to keep up the youthful appearance. The intern suspected she would regret it for exactly ten minutes, then remember why she'd said yes. Until the next morning anyway. Hangovers in your forties last for days.

On the couch, Noah and his roommate were asleep in a way that suggested that Noah was dreaming that his roommate was his ex-girlfriend. They were tangled together under a blanket Lily had quietly placed over them earlier, arms wrapped loosely, Noah's head rested on his roommates chest as if maybe he was the ex-girlfriend in this dream?

They would have questions later.

Thad had taken a photo.

"For accountability," he'd whispered to himself. "Or blackmail. Depending on my mood."

As the intern made his way through the house—stepping over shoes that didn't belong to anyone he could identify, navigating the aftermath of cups, cards, and abandoned laughter—he paused in the kitchen.

Lily was at the sink, washing the last few dishes slowly, deliberately, like this part mattered. The lights were low. Al Green played softly from a speaker on the kitchen counter.

Thad stood behind her, arms wrapped around her waist, chin resting lightly on her shoulder. They swayed together, barely moving, like the night had finally exhaled.

Neither spoke.

Thad looked up and caught the intern's eye as he was opening the front door.

He nodded once.

No words.

Just acknowledgment.

The intern nodded back and stepped outside.

The sky was clear. Stars were bright.

Poker night was over.

Work would return.

But not yet.

SATURDAY: "Just Monitoring"

The lie we tell ourselves.

11:30 AM — Minor Alert

The intern was scheduled to be primary on-call for the weekend. That meant waking up to check if something went wrong and hoping it didn't.

Their alarm had been set for 9:00 AM.

That didn't work out.

They didn't actually open their eyes until sometime after eleven, phone buzzing aggressively on the nightstand like it had been personally offended. They lay there for a moment, replaying fragments of the night before—cards, laughter, the pool, Thad midair—and Noah cuddling unknowingly with his roommate.

They had a slight headache, but not hungover.

They'd gone easy on the alcohol. One or two drinks. Enough to participate. Not enough to regret existence. This decision, would prove to be the best technical choice of the week.

There were no deployment or maintenance meetings on the calendar.

This was deliberate. Thad scheduled his poker nights outside of the regular release calendar.

These weekends were intended for recovery.

The intern opened their laptop to check on messages, emails, and alert monitors.

Teams was quiet.

Green dots flickered on and off.

Then an automated email alert arrived.

— — —

[Email]

Subject: WARNING - Elevated retry rate detected
Severity: Low
Status: Monitoring

— — —

The intern opened the dashboard, and squinted.

They checked logs. The workaround was still in place, layered carefully over the hotfix that had also been pushed the afternoon before. Retry patterns looked fine. Except where they didn't. Small spikes. Little blips. Nothing anyone else would notice.

They refreshed.

The alert stayed yellow.

Yellow meant *acknowledged. Don't touch it. Just watch it.*

Red would be when escalation was needed.

2:17 PM — Just Looking

The intern didn't message the channel.

They didn't open an incident.

They opened the runbook.

The runbook still referenced a system that no longer existed.

That was normal.

They followed it anyway in case there was some relevance to the current system.

Commands didn't line up. Variable names were wrong. One step referenced a server that had been decommissioned before the intern had been hired, possibly before they'd graduated.

They scrolled.

They adjusted mentally.

They made notes to follow with the team on later for making documentation updates.

3:15 PM — The Question They Didn't Ask

The monitor was still *yellow.*

The intern felt uneasy. They hovered over the keyboard.

They could escalate.

They knew exactly how that would go.

Someone would join half-awake and grumpy from a pounding headache.

Someone would ask if this was customer impacting.

Someone would ask who made the last change.

Someone would say *let's keep an eye on it.*

The dashboard would still be yellow and not red.

Nothing would change, except now it would be louder.

They closed Teams.

4:00 PM — The Fix That Isn't One

They tested a small adjustment in their own sandbox. While the intern couldn't make production changes, they could still test changes themselves to see what may happen in production.

Not really a fix or change.

More of a design suggestion.

They ran a load test against their sandbox. Traffic shifted just enough that the system didn't trip over itself.

The sandbox metric graphs responded.

Not dramatically.

No spike. No drop.

Just… smoother.

The alert disappeared in their sandbox environment.

The system settled.

The intern leaned back in their chair and stared at the ceiling for a moment, heart slowing.

They couldn't commit anything.

They just had to document it to lift up when the team was awake and willing to talk about work.

They took a screenshot and saved it to a folder labeled **References**, which was quietly becoming the most important folder on their laptop.

5:22 PM — Still Monitoring

Teams stirred.

— — —

[Teams | IT General]

Ortega, Sam (5:22 PM)
Anyone seeing anything weird?

Reynolds, Thad (5:22 PM)
You referring to work, or last night? ☺

Ortega, Sam (5:24 PM)
Ha, I don't know what you're talking about. Nothing happened last night.

— Reynolds, Thad reacted with 💯 —

— — —

The intern stared at the original message from Sam.

Then at the dashboard.

Then back at the message.

They typed.

Deleted.

Typed again.

Deleted again.

They added a reaction instead.

👀

A few seconds passed.

— Ortega, Sam reacted with 👍 —

That was enough.

6:00 PM — Silent Systems

The systems were quiet.

Not because they were healthy.

Because they were filled with duct tape and prayers.

The intern closed their laptop carefully, like it might break something on purpose if handled roughly. They didn't shut it hard. Didn't toss it aside. They placed it on the table with respect and backed away sarcastically.

At the office, the orange cones around the destroyed front lawn cast long shadows in the fading light. No one had moved them. No one would.

Inside, the hallways and cubes resembled a western ghost town. Not a soul to be found on the weekend. Anything that needed doing would be handled from home.

Saturday ended without incident.

SUNDAY: "Preparation Mode"

Anxiety in sweatpants.

10:42 AM — Not Working

No one said they were working.

There were no meetings. No alerts. No emails marked urgent. Teams was quiet in the way quiet rooms are quiet when everyone is listening for something.

The intern woke up later than usual and checked their phone anyway.

Nothing had happened.

This felt suspicious.

They put the phone face down, waited ten seconds, then flipped it back over.

Still nothing.

11:00 AM — The Pre-Monday Dread

By late morning, calendars were being reviewed quietly across the company.

Not edited. Reviewed. Mentally preparing.

People scrolled through Monday the way one scrolls through medical test results—slowly, already braced for bad news.

A meeting titled **Quick Alignment** had reappeared.

Duration: 30 minutes.

Attendees: Everyone.

The intern noticed they were still included.

They did not feel relieved.

12:14 PM — Drafts That Will Never Be Sent

As the intern continued to review monitors and logs, they drafted a few emails.

Some were deleted.

One began:

Just flagging something I noticed…

Delete.

Another started:

Not sure if this is relevant, but…

Delete.

The intern opened the postmortem again.

The owner was still **TBD**.

They closed it before TBD magically updated to their name.

1:37 PM — Quiet Maintenance

At the office, Jackie had driven in to check the cones on the front lawn.

The tape had been replaced. The grass had been measured. An estimate for additional landscaping work had been sent. Priority service caused a 50% increase in the estimate.

Inside, systems continued to run.

The workaround and hotfix remained in place.

It was now officially old enough to be called a permanent fix.

3:02 PM — Executive Weekend Email

The email arrived mid-afternoon, when people were least prepared to ignore it.

— — —

[Email]

From: Eugene
Subject: Hope You're Unplugging
Team,

Just wanted to say how proud I am of the way everyone handled last week.

I hope you're taking time today to unplug, reset, and recharge ahead of a strong start tomorrow.

Appreciate all you do.
—Eugene

Sent from iPhone.

— — —

The intern read it once.

Then again.

They wondered if anyone reading this on a weekend are actually unplugged at all.

They decided it didn't matter.

4:46 PM — Checking Anyway

The intern logged in again just to look.

The dashboards were now green.

The logs were quiet.

No alerts had fired.

Which meant the system was either stable or waiting.

Most likely due to less traffic on a Sunday, but a win is a win.

No one was called.

No changes were made by the team.

The intern logged out.

7:18 PM — Rituals

Dinner was eaten distractedly.

A show played in the background, unheard.

The intern glanced at Teams on their phone one more time while eating.

Thad had posted a single message earlier to **IT General**:

— — —

[Teams | IT General]

Reynolds, Thad (6:06 PM)
Tomorrow will be fine.

— — —

No one had reacted.

9:30 PM — The Calendar Invite

The notification arrived with the inevitability of gravity.

— — —

[Calendar Invite]

Subject: Quick Alignment
Time: Monday, 7:45 AM
Duration: 30 minutes
Agenda: Realignment

— — —

The intern accepted.

They did not consider declining.

They were expected to be tech support again.

Outside, it was dark.

The intern needed quality sleep to mentally prepare for another week. They had spent the day hydrating, to flush any party residue from their system.

Sunday ended without incident.

Which meant Monday could begin… again.

MONDAY (AGAIN): "Lessons Learned"

Nothing was learned.

Monday, 7:45 AM — Quick Realignment

I was walking through the door exactly 7:45 AM and took the side door mostly used by IT to prevent a lot of eyes noticing when people come and go. Unfortunately, that was the same time Eugene walked up to the door at the same time, as the elevator for this entrance dumped out right beside his office in the executive suite.

"Good morning. Happy Monday!" I said politely.

Eugene looked up from his cell phone, and checked my face, then badge, then a quick scan from head to toe to verify if he should know me, or care.

"Morning," he mumbled, quickly looking back down at his phone. No other words were spoken.

As we parted ways from the elevator, I took a long sip of my coffee that I had brought from home. This morning I switched up to a cinnamon roll flavored coffee, with a bit too much creamer, to make it feel more like a morning treat than the normal jump start fuel. As I walked past the breakroom, the sweet smell of my coffee mixed with the smell of ash tray water and burnt fish, triggering a mild gag reflex. I took a deep breath and rush passed to get to my desk. One of Jackie's minions were already standing by the coffee machine while wearing a mask that did nothing to prevent the smell. The machine had a sign next to it that red "Out of Order," as the minion navigated the inner workings to revive it for at least one more day.

By the time I reached my desk, I could smell grease and ash on my clothes as if the smell clung to me trying to escape the breakroom. I was the only one from IT at their desk, with only the offshore team being active from last night's testing and support work. The rest of the building showed little activity.

Online, execs were starting to show green on Teams, prepping for a call that was supposed to have already started. This week the focus shifted to a new priority: a client visit. There were references to a primary investor visiting as a follow-up to a regulatory review. Again, execs forwarded the call to their proxies to take notes, and accountability, for them.

At 7:50 AM, Eugene opened the call.

He **usually** joined early. It was less about being prepared, and more about symbolism. Being 5 minutes late implied shifting of priorities. To him, it suggested intention. To some of the others, is meant he wasn't very busy and could join whenever he felt like it. He had no time to look at himself on camera and make small adjustments. He failed to notice the racoon eye tan that resulted from a fresh coat of spray tan over the weekend. His salt and pepper hair still combed perfectly. He wore a different flavor of the same suit recipe. His teeth still shimmering in the camera light like smooth, glossy bathroom tiles.

"Apologies teams," he stated in a rushed tone. "I was chatting with a colleague from the investment firm that is planning to be here this week. I want to use this call to start the conversations for that visit. We can discuss last week's events later."

They would not be discussed later.

William had already joined the call. This was intentional. The investor that was visiting was a friend of his, and had driven the deal for the company. He did not speak. He mainly observed, and listened to ensure Eugene said what he wanted to hear.

The meeting title sat at the top of the screen:

Quick Alignment — Week Kickoff

15 minutes

No agenda. Only the impromptu topic just called out from Eugene. Eugene smiled once again at the empty grid, continually glancing down at himself in the lower corner of his screen.

With the notification that the meeting had started, the other execs started to roll in. At 7:52 AM, Bob, joined. Audio only.

"Mornin," Bob said.

"Good Morning! Happy Monday!" Eugene replied, brightly, as if he were being graded on it. Bob was already muted.

At 7:53 AM, Derrick joined from his phone.

"I'm here from my cell," Derrick stated, camera off, wind audible for a short bit until muted.

At 7:54 AM, Jessica appeared next, again, perfectly lit, neutral background, expression calibrated to empathy. Hair and makeup perfectly set. Clothing that looked professionally orchestrated. The twitch in her eye gone. Reset from the weekend release. This week she was a brunette.

Karen, the chief legal officer and general counsel, joined muted and off camera. Thad followed immediately behind her.

Barbara joined late, apologized in the chat again, and immediately began typing without muting her mic. The mic was muted much quicker this week, with Thad making it to the call before Barbara.

Eugene said. "Thank you to everyone for joining. Let's get started." The statement was followed by thumbs up reactions, but no other commentary.

Thad used this time on the call to multitask from his office. He checked in on his team and reviewed the dashboard for any weekend activity that needed his attention. The team was becoming more active on Teams, and talking about the great time on Friday at the place and event that would not be named.

"Alright," he said. "I really just wanted to assess our preparedness for this week's visitors before the day kicks off."

No comment from the crowd.

"What I'm focused on," Eugene continued, "is alignment."

Jessica nodded while still fully smiling.

"Specifically," Eugene said, "making sure we're all telling the same story as we head into another high-visibility week."

Karen unmuted.

"To whom?" she asked.

Eugene paused. He smiled the way people smile when buying time in public.

"That's a great question," he said.

This time he actually answered.

"We have a potential major investor coming this week, brought to us by William, and we need to make sure we leave them begging for more by the time they leave."

He then shared his screen.

He was presenting his calendar for about a minute too long, allowing the group to see a lot of blocked times with no actual meetings, many showing as being out of office. Once he realized he was sharing the wrong screen, he coughed, and quickly switched screens to the deck.

The title slide appeared:

FCCU_Investor_Narrative_DraftV2.pptx

Based on the slide format and the limited number of versions, the group could tell that Eugene did not create this deck. This was a product of William's. He knew what he wanted said, and how it needed it to be said.

"Can ya'll hear me speaking?" Barbara typed into chat.

No one commented. No one looked at chat.

By 8:15 AM, the group were now all fully aware that we investor would be on-site on Wednesday, expecting to see the demo that was just lifted up to the board the previous week. The deck was a product launch announcement, and demo to the investor as a "First to see" for what was coming. This time William needed to allocate responsibility, using Eugene as the puppet to deliver the message. Again, the participation increased once they realized they were being volunteered for the exposure. The group reviewed the slides, and agreed that the word **revolutionary** was a stretch. **Risks & Assumptions** felt honest but not a selling point. **Opportunity** felt vague and just an opportunity for unwanted question.

Thad cleared his throat.

"Before we align too tightly on messaging," he said, carefully, "I just want to remind the group that the demo was meant to be an internal soft launch on Wednesday to prep product teams for what's coming for a full deployment this weekend. If we demo to the investor on Wednesday instead, we are basically showing off vaporware."

The silence that followed was not confusion. It was avoidance.

"We will adjust as needed," William had unmuted to answer before Eugene could respond.

"Can you clarify what you mean by that?" Thad asked.

There was a pause. William did not intend to spend the time to explain his response.

"I'll follow up with you offline, Thad. We'll figure it out," a response from a windy cell phone from Derrick.

"Thanks, Derrick. That's what I like to hear," William added.

Thad stopped talking and went back on mute, knowing that Derrick was trying to help, but William just talked to him like tech support.

At 8:25 AM, Eugene glanced at the clock.

"Great call, gang," he said. "I'll let you get to your day."

The call ended.

Thirty seconds later, a Teams message appeared in the **IT General** channel.

— — —

[Teams | IT General]

Reynolds, Thad (8:25 AM)
Surprise! The demo scheduled for internal teams this Wednesday is now a live investor demo.

— Five people reacted with 👀 —

Brooks, Evan (8:26 AM)
WTF did you say?

— — —

No replies followed.

William leaned back in his chair. The week had officially started.

8:30 AM — Video Conferencing Is (Still) a Lie

The next meeting was scheduled for 8:30 AM. This time William did not attend. He had delegated what needed to be delegated, sounding almost as if it were an ultimatum. The subject of this call related to the new product feature demo that was intended to be a soft internal release, prior to full release at the end of the week.

At 8:29 AM, ten people joined.

At 8:30 AM, nothing happened.

At 8:31 AM, Eugene began speaking.

"Okay, looks like folks are still coming in," he said, speaking directly into the camera with the confidence of someone who assumed sound was a shared experience. "Can everyone hear me?"

Silence.

Then Derrick's voice cut through the wind noise.

"You're fine."

Eugene nodded. "Thanks."

He sat back getting a bit frustrated with Derrick calling in from a cell phone again. Did it make him look bad, allowing his subordinated work remote? Did he need to start work on the RTO mandates he had started drafting the week before?

Derrick was on-site with a client. It's part of his job.

"Good morning" Declan said as if already multitasking. "I'm on, but focusing on other items. Call my name if you need me."

Eugene's normal smile broke a bit. "Thanks for joining, Declan," he said, trying to cover the building frustration in his voice. Intrusive thoughts started to fill his head. *Do people not respect me? Is this why William was brought in?*

Bob unmuted long enough to claim participation. "I can hear everyone fine."

Jessica, along with Tom, were on and prepped for communications on the product launch. "Can I get a copy of the deck that was presented this morning?"

"Let me check with Tina and get it sent out," Eugene responded.

Karen typed something into the chat. No one read it.

Barbara raised her hand. Physically. On camera. Again.

"Barbara, go ahead," Eugene said.

"Am I unmuted?" Barbara asked herself before continuing.

She was.

"I wanted to verify that we have passed all compliance checks during testing, so we're good from our side," she said.

"Testing is still ongoing, since the plan was originally to push to staging for the internal demo on Wednesday," Evan chimed in, representing Thad. Thad was managing his own touchpoint calls for the product launch this week.

"Will we need to delay the demo to allow time to sign off testing?" Barbara responded.

Evan did not speak, as that decision was above his pay grade, compared to the execs on the call that could quickly override anything he would say.

"No, we will run parallel cycles with testing, while prepping for staging deployment. My product team will work with QA and IT, then follow up with compliance." Derrick responded. He knew enough tech speak to be dangerous, but savvy enough to calm the fears of execs thinking they wouldn't get their way. Thad would have been proud.

Thad joined late, once his own deployment timeline call had finished. Eugene was sharing closing remark slides. Thad missed the slides on the product status and action items. Once again, slides had been created without input from Thad, with no way to raise any objection to all of the things that could go wrong this week.

"Do we need to go back over any of the product deployment slides? I was handling the deployment calls with my teams, making sure to identify risks we are going to need to prep for," Thad asked.

"No, I think we are good, thanks. And quick housekeeping," Eugene said. "If you're not speaking, please mute."

Everyone muted. Even Barbara.

Eugene took a deep breath and continued speaking.

A calendar reminder chimed softly across the company. Somewhere in IT, the intern checked at a dashboard that was still green.

Green meant stable.

Yellow meant worry.

Red meant something was hitting the fan.

The dashboard did not change.

The meetings continued.

9:00 AM — Weekly Leadership Sync (Again)

The calendar said one hour.

Everyone knew that meant at least ninety minutes, possibly more if anyone asked a question that would result in an unintended action item.

By 8:59 AM, the grid was full again. The same faces, reordered slightly. Someone new occupied the "Rotating Middle Manager" square, introduced as "just helping keep us organized today," which meant they would be blamed later.

Eugene started on time.

William did not attend.

"Okay," he said, leaning forward. "Same as last week, I want to keep us tight and focused."

"Sounds good," Bob stated aggressively, which was his way of saying he was present.

"Let's start with finance," Eugene said. "Bob?"

Bob unmuted.

Bob began, "from a financial perspective, things are looking good on forecasts, assuming the expected numbers hit for the new product launch. We should see a decent increase in revenue based on previous quarter"

Bob didn't expand on anything. Vague. As intended.

He shared his screen. A spreadsheet appeared. It had not been updated since last Friday, as this master workbook for finance was maintained by Rachel Kim.

"Not much change since last week," Bob continued, "but nothing outside expected variance."

Bob had sat his large coffee mug on top of the resignation letter on his desk addressed to him, using it as a coaster. He had not noticed what it was.

"What were the numbers form the weekend? We normally see a 7-day history," Derrick asked.

Bob squinted. "Hard to tell. I can look more into it after the call."

Thad shifted slightly in his chair.

"Databases are all up and running fine. No issues over the weekend, so it shouldn't be a system issue," he said.

He was ignored. Again.

Bob did not look up. "We're don't normally see a material impact from the weekends. We should be fine."

The company saw the heaviest traffic on the weekends. They were a payment processing company. People shopped on the weekend. Bob knew this. *Or did he?*

The words *should be fine* landed quietly and stayed there.

Derrick leaned closer to his camera and pushed his sunglasses up on his forehead, pushing his sun bleached hair out of his face. "From a brand standpoint," he said, "I just want to make sure we're prepared if the investor notices anything on Wednesday."

"Notice what?" Eugene asked.

Thad smiled. "We'll take it offline, Derrick. We got this!"

The sarcasm was lost on everyone except Derrick, knowing his commentary just got thrown back at him. He smiled and went back on mute.

Jessica nodded thoughtfully. "It might be helpful to frame this as proactive communication," she said. "Just in case."

Karen unmuted. "We should not communicate anything unless we are certain it needs to be communicated."

Barbara cleared her throat.

"There is a regulatory expectation around any product release that impacts any regs," she said calmly. "Even for small impacts."

The silence that followed was longer this time.

"That's helpful context," Eugene said finally. "Let's take that offline."

Barbara wrote something down.

Thad tried again.

"We've tried rushing releases before based on clients coming in unexpectedly," he said. "When we do this, it usually uncovers gaps."

Long pause.

Bob glanced at the clock. "Do we know that it will?"

"No," Thad said. "But we know that it can."

Eugene nodded slowly, the way people nod when they are simply trying to buy time to come up with an executive response.

"Okay," he said. "Let's put a pin in this." Eugene pulled from his series of one-liners that could be used to deflect, redirect, or postpone any sort of accountability for an issue or concern.

The Rotating Middle Manager typed *STAY CLOSE* into the notes.

At 9:38 AM, the conversation drifted.

Declan was also on this call, again asked about headcount reduction opportunities based on the new product features and automation, followed by roadmap confidence.

"Will this new product allow us to see any headcount reduction benefit? We are still bloated in multiple areas." Declan inquired. He continued without pause, "And are we on track to hit production by Wednesday so that we start seeing the benefit?"

"Declan, I still feel good about the delivery timeline, but let's dig into the expense conversation later," Eugene responded.

"You said that last week. Again, what the hell is the point of new products and features that are supposed to make us more efficient if we can't talk about the expense benefits in the call about the product release?" Declan exclaimed like a broken record. He starts typing fiercely into a separate chat and goes on mute.

Derrick asked, " Since this was intended to be a soft launch internally this week, Will we at least be able to run the demo tomorrow, to ensure we are good for Wednesday?"

"So now we are trying to push even faster, to prep for a public deployment we weren't expecting to have?," Thad questioned, not expecting an answer. There was no response.

Thad stopped responding to questions and started responding to Teams.

In the **IT General** channel, the thread had grown.

— — —

[Teams | IT General]

Chen, Maya (9:40 AM)
What's the latest on the product rollout?

Natarajan, Priya (9:41 AM)
We haven't finished pre-deployment vulnerability scans yet.

Ortega, Sam (9:45 AM)
We have a few updates to push today based on the latest QA results.

Natarajan, Priya (9:48 AM)
So we'll have to rerun the scans before we can push?!

Reynolds, Thad (9:52 AM)
Not to add fuel to the fire, but exec is trying to push tomorrow to dry run before investor demo on Wednesday.

Brooks, Evan (9:53 AM)
WTD, Dude?! Stop going to meetings. You keep giving us worse news every time you attend one.

— Reynolds, Thad reacted with 💯 —

— Ortega, Sam reacted with 👍 —

— — —

At 10:04 AM, Eugene smiled again.

"I'm really encouraged by how cross-functional we continue to be," he said. "Great collaboration."

"I'll follow up with you and William offline to continue the headcount discussion," Declan added before immediately logging off the call. Eugene would be away from his desk when that call came.

Jessica went through some final communications talking points.

The meeting ran until 10:23 AM.

No decisions were made.

The group had seven minutes for a bio-break prior to the next call.

10:30 AM — (Another) Two-Hour Meeting That Could've Been an Email

The next meeting started with everyone on mute. Everyone felt that they were caught in some sort of time loop, that consisted of a weekly unnecessary urgent situation, self-made risks, and deaf executives that could only hear themselves speak.

The invite had been sent late Saturday evening from Tina with the only agenda being "alignment across teams for investor on-site visit." Attendance was high because everyone knew this meant being assigned responsibility for the executive-created emergency. The audience was the same as the previous leadership meeting, but expanded to also include the next level down and their proxies.

The Rotating Middle Manager spoke first.

"Thanks, everyone," they said. "The goal today is just to make sure we're all on the same page." The rotating manager seems to have been reading off of a script used by whomever had the rotating manager role for that specific call.

The page everyone was meant to be on was still vague.

Evan added Sam, both joining from their desks while multitasking on deployment tasks. Thad hovered in the camera background of their desks vs being presence at his own desk.

"So," Eugene said, appearing again, "I just want to reiterate that speed is really important right now for the new product launch. We intend to wow the investors on Wednesday."

That comment was the trigger for those on the call to understand what the new emergency was really about. *Executive ego and stakeholder value.* Those that had the meeting chat open saw a new list of individuals slowly being added to the call that had any relevant knowledge of the topic, or those that through they needed to be added as CYA. The attendee list went from 20 to 50 in a matter of minutes.

Evan nodded. "Realistically," he said, almost sarcastically mimicking himself from the previous week, "we can move quickly or we can move safely."

"Why not both?" Declan asked, not picking up on the sarcasm or realizing he continued to be a broken record from previous week.

Evan smiled, continuing the repeated dialogue.

"We can try," he said, hoping Declan would pick up on the tone.

Thad covered his mouth so as to not be seen smiling on camera, realizing what Evan was doing.

Luis, shared the same Jira board from last week. The ticket rainbow had shifted colors only slightly since last week. A little less than half of them were blocked.

"What's still blocking those?" Declan asked.

Luis glanced sideways. "Dependencies."

"On what?"

Luis paused. "Security vulnerability testing. QA Test patches that go out later today. Few other dependencies."

Thad did not attempt to chime in. He wasn't repeating last week's conversation.

"Remember, these are all priority #1, and all needed at the same time," Eugene stated, as if this should be a known fact already.

"Yup," Thad responded, "we are still waiting on the prioritization requests form Declan's operations leads. I have what I need form Derrick's team. Declan's team still has everything as priority #1, so, I will be assuming Derrick's priority order will be the source of truth unless the two teams come to agreement. I sent another set of requests via email and chat myself to Declan over the weekend asking for updates."

"I don't recall seeing anything related to this. We can take this offline and circle back," Declan responded. His face now blood red, again being put on the spot in an audience, now remembering this had been waiting on him for over a week. He would not admit that he did remember the conversation once Thad had reminded him.

This discussion was not written down in meeting notes by the rotating manager.

At 11:17 AM, Jessica asked whether communications could still go out prior to full deployment.

"Yes," Thad said immediately, "Comms won't change based on the items we are finishing up." Evan and Luis nodded in agreement.

Barbara spoke once more.

"If we continue to operate in this state," she said, "we will certainly shoot ourselves in the foot."

"Thank you again, Barbara," Thad responded. Barbara seemed to slowly become a fan of Thad for continuing to acknowledge her participation in calls.

Eugene nodded. "Totally hear that."

Nothing changed.

At 12:32 PM, Eugene looked at the clock.

"Ok," he said. "Good discussion."

No priorities were established. No confirmation on early deployment was achieved.

The meeting ended at 12:34 PM.

Four people remained on the call anyway, with cameras off, because they had walked away for lunch and let the meeting stay up on their machine.

This entire feature rollout status could have been a status summary email. More meetings like this would follow.

1:00 PM — Lunch That Is Almost Lunch

This calendar invite came at 10:45 AM from Thad's cell phone for a working lunch that he was trying to avoid. The IT team members were to huddle in the IT Conference room, while others were allowed to work from their desks if needed, but all were invited to sit with IT if they wanted.

— — —

[Calendar Invite]

Subject: Working Lunch (Sorry)
Duration: 120 minutes
Agenda: New Product Deployment & Communication Logistics
Description: This is a working session to make sure that we are prepared for a an early deployment for the product release. I will need to have folks from communications, call center operations, and product team to join us to make sure we have a proper runbook created for step-by-step activity.

PS: If you are joining me in the IT Conference room, I will feed you.

— — —

IT had the best junk food, and Thad always ordered good food for his working sessions. He hated keeping people in the office for their lunch hour, but the situation demanded alignment so that the self-inflicted damages the company would put on themselves would be a minimal as possible. There was a counter along the side of the IT Conference room that was always stocked with chips, sodas, candy, and even those zero calorie energy drinks and flavored waters for those trying to watch their weight. Today Thad had pizza and doughnuts delivered from two local shops that the department would visit often. Thad had become friends with the owners of both shops, and their goods were far from any franchise pizza joints or bakeries. Freshly made, hefty portions, abundant in calories. He also ordered a variety of salad bowls for those that didn't want to eat something heavy. There would be people in food comas before close of business.

The thought of **good** free food brought in others from outside of IT. Knowing that others would come, the IT team made their plates quickly so as to get enough before the vultures picked off the remaining slices and doughnuts.

At 12:58 PM, people started walking in, and joining on the conference room TV. By 1:05 PM, the IT team had their plates made and laptops open to start reviewing deployment steps. The remaining attendees continued to roll in, with the final attendees being from the call center that had to wait until a specific group of agents could come off of the phones to attend the call. The three agents who walked in first were in their early twenties. All young attractive females hired right out of college. Following them came the senior manager of the call center – Randall Jenkins.

Randall was a walking HR violation. Early fifties. Heavy set, balding, with a salt and pepper beard. He wore think, black framed bifocals, that he continually had to pull to the end of his nose to see anything farther than 5 feet away from him. His wardrobe composed primarily of V-Neck sweaters, with no undershirt, baggy jeans, held up by a belt that disappeared beneath the belly overlap. The look was completed with orthopedic shoes in a variety of colors from black, to gray, to white, to more gray. He had a 5 o'clock shadow by 1 o'clock, and normally some form of food stain on his shirt from that day's breakfast or lunch. He was the sole user of the coffee machine in the break room when it worked.

He had hired these call center agents, and rows of others that looked just like them. They walked in at a distance from Randall, and tried to find seats opposite from him at the conference room table. As they sat down with their plates, he walked slowly behind them, leaning over, "Hey Sweetie, can I fit in here between you all?"

"There's not enough room for another seat, Randall," one of the girls said sternly.

With a hurt puppy dog look, Randall found a place at the end of the table, beneath the conference room TV that people often avoided to prevent everyone looking at them. He hunched over his plate of pizza and doughnuts, barely breathing between bites to avoid wasting precious chewing time.

Jessica was already in the room, and watch the exchange, as the hair on the back of her neck stood on edge. She had a folder as thick as an encyclopedia in her office on Randall. Constant complaints of shoulder massages, inappropriate jokes, and aggressive conversation with his subordinates. Complaints that were consistently ignored or swept over by Declan who didn't have time for "HR nonsense." It would take a blatant legal infraction to make him pay attention. She took a deep breath and joined in on the current meeting.

"Hi everyone," she said warmly. "Thank you for inviting Tom and me to the session, and thank you for the salad!" Thad knew which salad was her favorite, and had already put it to the side for her.

"Yeah, thank you for the invite, and glad to see Jessica and Communications here," Randall chimed in as he looked at Jessica and winked. She looked away quickly as she felt a small gag reflex trigger. The uncomfortable feeling was shared by everyone in the room. This would not be the last cringy exchange with Randall this week.

"Ok gang, we don't have much time," Thad started. "We are now apparently on the hook to get the new product set to at least the staging environment by tomorrow to have a dry run prior to investors being here on Wednesday. I want to go through deployment steps, followed by the communication plan, and end with the call center operations runbook for the new features, and calls that may come in from customers and clients for support. We expect a good bit of added call volume."

Everyone nodded in agreement, since Thad was always good at creating a clear purpose for the group, and making everyone feel like they had an important role. It was the complete opposite of meetings held be the other execs.

Derrick had joined the meeting from his tablet, sitting in a hotel while visiting a different client for the day. "Thank you for putting this together, Thad," he said. "Just let me know what my team needs to prep for any discussions with the client."

Thad nodded.

For the next two hours, the team walked through runbooks, drafts for communications to customers and clients, status on vulnerability scans for the latest deployment to the QA environment, and FAQ Updates for the call center to be prepared for. The call center agents were fully engaged, eager to learn and contribute, so that maybe they would be seen as great additions to other teams instead of reporting to Randall. Randall simply looked at them and winked when they spoke, then looked back at his phone throughout the meeting.

Jessica put on a cracked smiled.

"Just another reminder," she said gently, "that professionalism applies in all settings, including informal ones."

Thad smirked.

Randall was clueless.

"And," she emphasized, hoping he would get the hint, "just remember that we should all be mindful of optics. Especially when the investors arrive."

Still nothing. Randall continued to scroll social media.

At 1:15 PM, Declan joined virtually. "Why am I on this call?"

"This was more of an FYI for you that it was taking place. You were set as optional," Thad responded.

Randall dropped his phone as if it were on fire. It fell to the floor. He did not move to pick it up.

"Randall, do you have this covered?" Declan asked.

"Yes, sir. I've got us covered," he responded.

Declan dropped before he finished the response.

At 1:25 PM, a Teams notification pinged across several screens.

— — —

[Teams | Company Announcements]

Facilities (1:25 PM)
Reminder: Please reserve conference rooms and huddle rooms accurately and vacate promptly after meetings. The board room currently has scheduled meetings that will be cancelled to make room for investors coming on site.

— — —

Tina had asked Jackie to send that notification.

There were no reactions. There we a myriad of reactions across separate, private chats.

At 1:26 PM, Jessica spoke again.

"It feels like we can use this time to also level set the teams on behavior expectations during the investor visit. Randall can you please be sure your teams have their respective areas clean, all confidential paperwork and materials are put away, they are in business casual attire, and conversations are professional and work related."

She paused, hoping for a response from Randall. He winked and casually responded, "Sure thing." He did not feel that the remark was intended for him but would convey it to his teams.

"If anyone has questions," she said, "my door is always open."

This was not intended for Randall. Her door, nor her calendar, were open. If her team needed to talk or file a complaint, she would make time.

At 1:45 PM, the meeting ended early.

Several people stayed on the call anyway, using the time blocked on their calendar to as cover to prevent being added to other impromptu meetings.

In a different channel, someone typed:

Did you see Randall in that meeting?

No one replied.

The working lunch was over. Work was actually accomplished. Many would now take a quick 15-30 minute nap in the parking lot to help digest pizza and doughnuts.

3:00 PM — Compliance Says Hi (Again)

Barbara sent an email.

She had considered a Teams message and decided against it.

— — —

[Email]

From: Hensley, Barbara

Subject: Compliance Impacts for Product Launch

Hi all,

Flagging a potential compliance reporting issue related to the new product feature launch this week. This is likely manageable if addressed promptly. I'd be happy to discuss.

Best,
Barbara Hensley
Chief Compliance Officer

— — —

No one replied.

Thad rolled his eyes.

This was not minor.

3:12 PM — Meanwhile, in Reality (Again)

By 3:12 PM, Thad and his team had stopped attending meetings.

This was not a decision so much as capacity constraints. All focus on premature product deployment.

He was still present everywhere he was expected to be. Teams red dot active as "Busy," calendar blocks intact, but his team's attention had shifted to the only current priority.

Vulnerability scanning finally completed, with a series of items that had to be corrected before the code could be deployed.

The list of vulnerabilities had almost tripled since before the last QA patch.

Thad checked the deployment logs for who committed the last build.

Noah.

Noah had pushed a series of updates in the latest build that he had "written" with the help of an AI assistant. The term *help* was defined in this case as pure **vibe coding**. Thad was not aware that he was using the assistant, as the company was still in a pilot phase, and he had told his team not to use it on code intended to move to production.

Priya noticed first and posted to a private chat with Luis, Evan, and Thad.

— — —

[Teams | Private Chat]

Natarajan, Priya (3:12 PM)
Vulnerability scan completed. Tripled the number of items found. WTH Happened?

Alvarez, Luis (3:12 PM)
I'm chatting with Noah currently. He pushed the last change to QA.

Alvarez, Luis (3:15 PM)
Uum… bad news.
He used the AI Assistant and vibe coded this change package.

Reynolds, Thad (3:16 PM)
Excuse me?

Natarajan, Priya (3:16 PM)
How? We blocked that to only sandbox usage.

Alvarez, Luis (3:18 PM)
Yeah. Coded, exported, imported, deployed.
Basically copy and paste.
He said he used the assistant to also run vulnerability scans on it, so he thought it was solid.

Reynolds, Thad (3:20 PM)
Geezus Kriste, people. We are getting creative with how we step on our own toes lately.
Let me open a channel to discuss as a group.

— — —

Thad maximized Teams and created a new channel, "**Deployment War Room – Lite**," inviting his Tech and

Security teams. That name still mattered. Calling it only a war room would have triggered visibility and immediate forwarding and escalations as the normal CYA protocol. *Lite* suggested more curiosity than urgency.

People joined without being invited.

Sam was already typing.

— — —

[Teams | Deployment War Room – Lite]

Patel, Noah (3:25 PM)
I'm so sorry. I can back out the build.
But it means we go back to the original build with the existing vulnerabilities.
I thought it was solid.

Reynolds, Thad (3:28 PM)
Back it out now. The Priya's group will rerun scanning. We need to ensure:
1) It doesn't get pushed any higher
2) We don't have to explain the added delay to my cohorts yet.

— Natarajan, Priya reacted with 👍 —

— — —

No one disagreed.

3:26 PM — A Reasonable Question

The Intern was in the channel.

They were intentionally invited this time to help document and suggest remediations.

They had been reviewing deployment logs and documentation related to the new product features. The runbook was newly updated, and was very detailed by Noah and Luis, which made it trustworthy.

Something didn't align.

They scrolled back through historical changes in the runbooks. Then further. Then further still.

After deleting and retyping twice, they posted.

— — —

[Teams | Deployment War Room – Lite]

Intern (3:35 PM)
Quick question… are we expecting all of these additional methods, JavaScript files, and new references that are have been added in the latest build?

— The channel paused. —

Patel, Noah (3:38 PM)
Not really. It was created based on the prompt I had used for the new features.

Alvarez, Luis (3:39 PM)
Why did the AI add all of this unnecessary garbage just to add the few things you asked for?
Did you not question the amount of code it spit out for the small request you made?

Patel, Noah (3:38 PM)
Not really. It explained why it made it all and sounded logical to me. I even asked it to security scan itself to any new vulnerabilities," Noah responded.

Reynolds, Thad (3:40 PM)
Noah, we went through this when we first opened up AI for use in sandbox. It was not meant for live code on real products.
You've also only been here a year, and right out of college. There are peer review processes in place for a reason. This should have gone through Luis, or at least a senior developer for review first.

Patel, Noah (3:42 PM)
I'm so sorry.

— — —

Noah lost his girlfriend as told at the party, and now may be losing his job.

3:45 PM — Controlled Panic

This scenario was preventable.

A failure in process.

Now it was time for remediation.

Escalate too early and executive leadership intervenes.

Namely Eugene, Declan, and William.

Escalate too late and leadership asks why no one spoke up.

Luis proposed a workaround.

— — —

[Teams | Private Chat]

Alvarez, Luis (3:45 PM)
I can roll back to the previous build, and also comment out a feature or two that was causing the most vulnerability items. We can then do an emergency push next week after the dust settles on the demo.

Reynolds, Thad (3:46 PM)
How many vulnerabilities would remain?

Natarajan, Priya (3:46 PM)
And what is the severity of the remaining items?

Alvarez, Luis (3:48 PM)
Not 100% sure yet, but it would be a fraction of the current list, and may buy us some time.

Reynolds, Thad (3:49 PM)
Get started on the rollback, and Priya, be ready for another scan. We may be working a bit late today.

— Natarajan, Priya reacted with 👍 —

Reynolds, Thad (3:49 PM)
Noah, you will be responsible for the RCA process that we will document and track internally.

— Patel, Noah reacted with 👍 —

Natarajan, Priya (3:50 PM)
Noah, document everything.
Especially the decision to do this. I'll need a change ticket to approve from a security standpoint for additional scans.

Patel, Noah (3:51 PM)
I'm so sorry. I thought I was being efficient.
I will do better.

Reynolds, Thad (3:52 PM)
This is a definite learning opportunity for all of us.

— — —

Thad knew how this would age.

4:08 PM — Executive Update (Draft)

While Luis ran the rollback, Thad opened a document titled:

Executive Update — Draft

He deleted three versions before keeping the fourth.

— — —

[Document]

Summary

Teams are working continued vulnerability items for the product code that needs to be deployed. No confirmed deployment impact at this time. Mitigations are in progress.

Thad – CTO

— — —

He stared at it.

Too specific.

He revised.

— — —

[Document]

Summary

We are monitoring remaining security assessment items tied to the upcoming product feature release. Deployment schedule for the staging environment remain on track. Teams are aligned on next steps.

Thad – CTO

— — —

He shared it in the channel.

Priya reacted with 👍

Noah removed a reaction he hadn't meant to add.

5:32 PM — Stability Achieved

The rollback completed and reduced features were reduced that also reduced the list of vulnerabilities.

Testing continued with no new vulnerabilities found.

Deployment could happen tomorrow.

Thad could speak around the reduced features as if it were intentional.

Which meant the story was now optional.

Thad sent a direct message.

— — —

[Team | Private Message]

Reynolds, Thad (5:32 PM)
We will need to chat tomorrow, and walk through everything leading up to today. Don't stress over it tonight. You're not fired or anything. But we will need to come up with a plan of prevention, lessons learned, and you will help me prevent others from making the same mistake.

Patel, Noah (5:33 PM)
Yes, sir.
Whatever you need me to do, just let me know.

Thad reacted with 👍

Reynolds, Thad (5:35 PM)
Again, please don't stress on it. I know that is easier said than done when I'm the one telling you this, but it will be fine.

Noah reacted with 👍

— — —

No one else would know about this conversation. There was no need to embarrass or call anyone out for a learning opportunity.

7:45 PM — Postmortem Draft #1

Noah stayed late.

The postmortem appeared in the shared drive at 7:45 PM.

It was labeled **DRAFT**, but being for the IT team internally, it would be updated the next day with further details.

— — —

[Document]

Incident Summary

Extensive vulnerabilities introduced by AI Assisted product feature code package deployment

Impact

- Minimal. QA Environment Only.
- Delay in Info Sec and QA cycles.
- No externally exposed vulnerabilities.

Root Cause

Multiple contributing factors related to internal AI assisted development activity.

Detection

Identified through security vulnerability scanning

Response

Teams collaborated to roll back deployment, and reduce problematic code in the prior release.

What Went Well

- Internal IT Team Collaboration
- Rapid response
- Effective communication from executive IT leadership

What Could Be Improved

- Change visibility
- Process clarity
- Training adherence
- Tighter AI Assisted Code Restrictions

Action Items

- Review sandbox access controls for AI Assistant
- Update runbooks
- Improve monitoring granularity

Owner

Noah Patel

— — —

Noah read it twice.

They felt every sentence.

He felt his name should be in a larger font so that everyone knew he accepted the responsibility. He notified the team that the document was uploaded.

At 8:03 PM, Thad reacted to the Teams update with a thumbs-up.

At 8:15 PM, Priya stated that the latest scans came back cleaner, with no critical or high vulnerabilities found. It would pass muster for deployment to Staging for the demo. That could wait until morning.

As Noah was leaving, he walked through the call center to exit out the main entrance. Call center agents were still taking calls, as they did not close until 9:00 PM. Noah waved at a few friends that had graduated from the same college and wound up at the same company. He noticed Randall was still at work, walking the aisles of his agents, listening in on calls. Randall didn't notice Noah walking by and proceeded to lean over one of his agents, put his hands on her shoulders and start to get her a massage. Her face clinched waiting for it to be over. She leaned forward to get out of his grip, grab her purse, and start to shut down her machine to head home. Randall then noticed Noah looking and rush back to his office as if he had definitely just gotten caught.

9:00 PM — Fade Out (For Real This Time)

Calendars filled.

Teams pings resumed.

The dashboards stayed green.

Deployment build was ready.

The lawn was still roped off. Pallets of grass and bushes still spread out on the side of the lawn, ready to be laid.

Inside the system, everything looked stable.

Which meant it would hold.

For now.

Monday ended the way it began.

With frustration.

With meetings.

With the quiet understanding that nothing essential had changed—only the language around it.

The calendar reminder chimed softly.

Another **Quick Alignment** had been scheduled.

No one declined.

EPILOGUE

The internship ended at the end of that week, as scheduled.

This was communicated via email. It included a brief thank-you, a request to return my badge, and a link to an exit survey. The subject line referenced *next steps*, though there were none.

The survey asked whether the experience had met my expectations.

I selected **Mostly**.

There was a question about whether I felt adequately supported.

I marked **Definitely**.

By the time I finished the rest of the form, the week's events had already been reclassified internally. It appeared in documentation as a *learning experience*. The decks had been updated. The language had improved. Several action items were marked complete.

I recognized some of them.

The systems were still operational. The dashboards were green. I now understood that green meant *resilient*, which was better than *accurate*. There were fewer meetings on the calendar, though a few had been rescheduled for the following quarter under different names.

One of them was called **Quick Alignment**.

I returned my badge on a Friday afternoon. The security desk thanked me and wished me luck. Jackie waved goodbye as I walked out to the parking lot. The team had said their goodbyes and thank you's via Teams prior to shutting down the laptop the last time and turning it in to support. No one asked any questions.

I did learn a lot.

Not in the way the onboarding deck promised. Better.

I learned where money pauses before it moves.

I learned how responsibility shifts without changing hands.

I learned which risks are documented and which ones are managed socially.

I learned that anything labeled *temporary* should be assumed permanent unless proven otherwise.

I learned that what happens on the calendar matters less than what happens between meetings.

These felt like useful things to know.

I took note on how effective leaders treat people, and documented what not to do based on how poor leaders treated their people.

The exit survey confirmed that my responses had been recorded. It mentioned that someone might follow up if clarification was needed.

No one did.

A week later, I received an automated message inviting me to apply again in the future. The company is always looking for curious, adaptable people who thrive in complex environments.

I believed that. At least in the IT department.

I still have my notes.

I don't plan to use them, but it felt weird to delete them entirely. You never know when they might be useful again, especially in companies that prefer to remember selectively.

If there's ever another week like this one, I'll probably recognize it sooner.

I'm not sure whether that's reassuring.

But it should help.

APPENDIX A: The Organizational Chart (Unofficial)

(How the company actually functions)

Personal Note: This organizational chart seems to change without notice, explanation, or measurable impact.

<u>Board of Directors</u>
Robert DuFray – Chairman of the Board / Owner

- Officially reports to: Shareholders
- Actually reports to: His assistant, Nancy
- Thinks in dollars, not sentences
- Likes being important
- Ignores any answer that isn't 'yes.'

<u>Executive Leadership</u>
Eugene Caldwell — Co-CEO

- Officially reports to: The Board
- Actually reports to: William Ashford
- Runs meetings, not outcomes
- Extremely positive about bad situations
- Uses "alignment" when a decision is being avoided
- Will delegate someone else instead of answering

William Ashford — Co-CEO

- Officially reports to: The Board
- Actually reports to: Robert DuFray
- Speaks in vision, not specifics
- Rarely in meetings, always referenced in them
- Messages flow downward, clarity does not

Declan "Dex" O'Rourke — COO

- Officially reports to: Eugene Caldwell
- Actually reports to: William Ashford

- Loud, effective, slightly terrifying
- Executes decisions without asking many questions
- Appears to tolerate Eugene as part of the job

Barbara Hensley — Chief Compliance Officer

- Officially reports to: Karen Whitaker
- Actually reports to: Karen Whitaker
- Calm, sincere, consistently ignored
- Becomes relevant only after something breaks
- Has a lot of trouble with using technology

Jessica Lane — Chief People Officer

- Officially reports to: Eugene Caldwell
- Actually reports to: Karen Whitaker
- Handles feelings before consequences
- Delivers bad news gently
- Language is soft; outcomes are not
- Seems to be on the brink of a meltdown

Karen Whitaker — General Counsel

- Officially reports to: William Ashford
- Actually reports to: The Board
- Controls language after incidents
- Communicates directly, thoroughly, and slowly
- Silence usually means "don't write that"

Bob Mercer — Chief Financial Officer

- Officially reports to: Eugene Caldwell
- Actually reports to: Eugene Caldwell
- Measures everything in dollar amounts
- Treats people like variables
- Always has a chart that isn't update by him

Derrick Vaughn — Chief Marketing Officer

- Officially reports to: William Ashford

- Actually reports to: William Ashford
- Launches messaging before products exist
- Extremely optimistic
- Reality is more of a suggestion

<u>**Technology & Security**</u>

Thad Reynolds — Chief Technology Officer

- Officially reports to: Eugene Caldwell
- Actually reports to: the entire executive committee
- Usually right, rarely listened to
- Gets looped in late, blamed early
- Very likeable. Everyone seems to follow his lead

Priya Natarajan — Sr. Director, Information Security

- Officially reports to: Thad Reynolds
- Actually reports to: Thad Reynolds
- Calmly explains alarming things
- Documents everything
- Has already warned everyone, in writing

Maya Chen — Director of Infrastructure

- Officially reports to: Thad Reynolds
- Actually reports to: Thad Reynolds
- Keeps systems alive with duct tape and hope
- Knows which systems cannot be touched
- "Temporary" fixes are very old

Luis Alvarez — Director of Applications

- Officially reports to: Thad Reynolds
- Actually reports to: Jira Boards
- Translates ideas into tickets
- Filters executive chaos
- Lives in backlog grooming

__Engineering & Development__

Evan Brooks — Engineering Manager

- Officially reports to: Luis Alvarez
- Actually reports to: Thad Reynolds
- Shields engineers from leadership
- Reframes impossible deadlines
- Uses curse words in IM's a lot

Sam Ortega — Senior Engineer

- Officially reports to: Evan Brooks
- Actually reports to: Evan Brooks
- Prevents disasters without telling anyone
- Cynical but competent
- "Temporary" fixes never revert

Noah Patel — Junior Developer

- Officially reports to: Evan Brooks
- Actually reports to: Evan Brooks
- Follows instructions literally
- He means well
- Needs to learn how to slow down

__Finance & Analytics__

Alex Donnelly — Sr. Director of Finance

- Officially reports to: Bob Mercer
- Actually reports to: Bob Mercer
- Turns chaos into numbers
- Corrects mistakes quietly
- Fashionista
- Morale gray area. Makes HR nervous

Rachel Kim — Senior Financial Analyst

- Officially reports to: Alex Donnelly
- Actually reports to: Bob Mercer
- Makes decks look intentional
- Rebuilds models overnight

- Re-runs numbers until they're acceptable
- Underappreciated by Bob.

<u>**Marketing & Communications**</u>

Lily Harper — Content Manager

- Officially reports to: Derrick Vaughn
- Actually reports to: Derrick Vaughn
- Publishes optimism
- Schedules posts during outages
- Quiet, but seems to be liked by IT.

<u>**People & HR Operations**</u>

Emily Foster — HR Business Partner

- Officially reports to: Jessica Lane
- Actually reports to: Jessica Lane
- Explains executive decisions to humans
- Very empathetic, very constrained
- Says "I wish I had more context" often

Michael Reeves — Talent Program Manager

- Officially reports to: Jessica Lane
- Actually reports to: Jessica Lane
- Owns programs no one completes

Tom Willis — Director of Communications

- Officially reports to: Jessica Lane
- Actually reports to: Derrick Vaughn
- Makes bad news sound aspirational
- Always asks, "What's the approved wording?"

The Rotating Middle Manager (Unnamed)

- Officially reports to: Everyone
- Actually reports to: Everyone Else
- Takes notes that become action items for others
- Pushes pressure downward, optimism upward

- Never the same person. Not sure where they came from

<u>**Operations**</u>

Randall Jenkins — Senior Manager, Call Center Operations

- Officially reports to: Declan O'Rourke
- Actually reports to: Declan O'Rourke
- Walking HR violation
- Calls every woman "Sweetie." Ignores men entirely
- Very handsy.

Jordan Feldman — Business Analyst (Ops)

- Officially reports to: Director of Change Management
- Actually reports to: Director of Change Management
- Translates English into flowcharts
- Frequently says "per my last diagram"
- Cares more about women, protein, and working out, than work.

Final Note

***This chart should not be referenced during meetings, performance reviews, or legal proceedings. My notes only.*

APPENDIX B: Glossary of Corporate Phrases (Unofficial)

Alignment

Agreement without commitment

Circle Back

Permanent deferral disguised as action

Quick Sync

Any meeting longer than promised

Visibility

The appearance of control

Lean Operating Model

Fewer people, same expectations

Safe Space

A room where no real answers are given

Offline

Never

Action Items

Someone else's future problem

High Priority

Emotionally urgent, operationally optional

Stakeholder

Anyone who can stop progress without fixing anything

Roadmap

A guess presented as a plan

Payments & Fintech Terms

Authorization

A temporary "yes" that may become a "no"

Settlement

Something that happens later, allegedly

Funds Availability

A flexible concept

Real-Time Payments

Near real-time, with exceptions

Reconciliation

Finding out the numbers were never going to match

Intermittent Latency

We noticed it before you did (maybe)

Fraud Mitigation

Blocking good customers to stop bad actors

Chargeback

A problem that arrives months after the decision

Technology Terms

Theoretically Scalable

Works great in slides

Legacy System

Critical, untouchable, undocumented

Technical Debt

Temporary, according to leadership

Hotfix

Permanent Change

Modernization

Always six months away

Single Source of Truth

Several Sources of truth referenced at the same time

High Availability

Until it isn't

***Definitions subject to change following the next meeting.*

APPENDIX C: Vision and Values

(As Displayed on the Careers Page)

Our Vision

To be a values-led, customer-focused organization that delivers meaningful outcomes through alignment, accountability, and thoughtfully managed expectations.

Core Values

Integrity

We do the right thing—even when it's inconvenient, delayed, or quietly redefined.

Transparency

We believe in open communication, especially when information is abstracted, summarized, or withheld for clarity.

Customer Obsession

Our customers are at the center of every decision, except internal ones.

Bias for Action

We move quickly once alignment has been achieved.

Ownership

We empower teams to take accountability, provided approvals are secured in advance.

One Team

We succeed together and fail in silos.

Resilience

We adapt, persevere, and schedule retrospectives.

APPENDIX D: Press Release

FOR IMMEDIATE RELEASE

Applied Systems, Inc. (ASYS) Announces Upcoming Platform Enhancements to Advance Payment Experiences

New capabilities designed to improve flexibility, performance, and future-ready scalability

[Franklin] — Applied Systems, Inc. (ASYS), a leading fintech innovator committed to shaping the future of digital payments, today announced a series of upcoming enhancements to its payments platform, reinforcing its continued focus on innovation, reliability, and customer-centric growth.

These enhancements, currently in the final stages of readiness, are designed to deliver improved responsiveness, expanded functionality, and a more seamless experience across key payment workflows. Customers can expect incremental improvements that support evolving transaction needs while laying the groundwork for additional capabilities in future releases.

"Our platform continues to evolve in meaningful ways," said William Ashford, Co-CEO of ASYS. "These enhancements reflect our ongoing investment in resilient technology and our commitment to delivering value through thoughtful, forward-looking improvements."

ASYS noted that the updates are the result of close collaboration across engineering, product, and operations teams, ensuring alignment with both customer expectations and long-term platform strategy.

"We're excited about the progress being made," added Derrick Vaughn, the company's Chief Marketing Officer. "This release represents another step forward in our continuous journey toward operational excellence and scalable innovation."

The company emphasized that these enhancements are part of its regular platform evolution and will be introduced in phases, with additional details to be shared as capabilities become available.

For more information, customers are encouraged to contact their account representatives or visit asysusa.com.

About Applied Systems, Inc. (ASYS)

ASYS is a mission-driven fintech organization focused on innovation, trust, and scalable growth. By leveraging advanced technology and deep industry expertise, the company partners with customers to support secure, reliable, and forward-looking payment solutions in an ever-changing financial landscape.

Media Contact:
press@asysusa.com

www.ingramcontent.com/pod-product-compliance
Lightning Source LLC
Chambersburg PA
CBHW070745180626
46818CB00007B/2997